FRIEND OR FOE?

"I hope the wars are over, my friend," General Crook said to Geronimo, facing him across the desk. "I hope the Apaches and the White-eyes can live in peace from here on. Nantan Lupan wants the Apaches to learn to be farmers. It's their only chance. They must change. The old days are gone."

While Crook was talking, Geronimo had decided that the meeting was over. He didn't want to hear the general talk about the need for Apaches to learn to be farmers. They had always been farmers, but Geronimo knew what Nantan Lupan meant. He meant that he wanted them to learn to be farmers the way that white men were farmers. He pretended not to be listening, and he turned as if to leave the room, but he paused for a moment, facing Lieutenant Gatewood.

"Gatewood," he said, "will you come and visit me at Turkey Creek?"

Gatewood studied the hard, dark face there in front of him for a moment, the face of a man he had said he wanted to kill, the face of a man who had killed his friends. But it was also now the face of a man who had fought by his side.

"Yes," he said. "I would like that."

And the lieutenant was surprised to find that he actually meant what he had said. Had he also been looking into the face of . . . a friend?

Books by Robert J. Conley

Geronimo: An American Legend* (Movie Tie-In)
The Way South
The White Path
The Long Trail North*
The Dark Way
Border Line*
The Way of the Priests
Mountain Windsong: *A Novel of the Trail of Tears*
Nickajack
Ned Christie's War*
Strange Company*
Go-Ahead Rider*
Quitting Time*
The Saga of Henry Starr
Colfax
Wilder and Wilder
The Witch of Goingsnake *and Other Stories*
Killing Time
Back to Malachi
The Actor
The Rattlesnake Band *and Other Poems*

*Published by POCKET BOOKS

GERONIMO
— AN AMERICAN LEGEND —

**A Novel by Robert J. Conley
Based on a Story by John Milius
Screenplay by John Milius and Larry Gross**

POCKET BOOKS

New York   London   Toronto   Sydney   Tokyo   Singapore

An *Original* Publication of POCKET BOOKS

POCKET BOOKS, a division of Simon & Schuster Inc.
1230 Avenue of the Americas, New York, NY 10020

ISBN: 0-671-88982-6

First Pocket Books printing January 1994

10 9 8 7 6 5 4 3 2 1

POCKET and colophon are registered trademarks of Simon & Schuster Inc.

Printed in the U.S.A.

Introduction

Geronimo was born in what is now the state of Arizona, in June of 1829, the fourth of a family of four boys and four girls, in the Bedonkohe band of Apaches. According to Geronimo himself, the Apaches, who called themselves Dineh (the People), were divided into four bands: the Bedonkohe, the Chokonen, the Chihenne, and the Nedni. The Chokonen lived south of the Bedonkohe, and the two groups were closely associated. The great leader of the Chokonen during Geronimo's youth was Cochise. White people knew the Chokonen as the Chiricahuas, the Bedonkohe as Mescalero.

Geronimo's name, in Apache, was Gokhlaye, and in 1846, at the age of seventeen, he was admitted to the Council of Warriors. The chief of the Bedonkohe at that time was the great Mangas Colorado.

The Apaches are said to have been nomadic. Probably, seminomadic would be a more accurate designation. Each band had its own territory, recognized and respected by the others. They were hunters, but they were also farmers, growing annual crops of corn, melons, pumpkins, and beans. Villages and cultivated fields were moved about from time to time within the recognized territory of the band. They were mountain people, but they also knew well the surrounding desert country, for in the winter they moved down to the desert for warmth.

They were also raiders, and the name Apache was given to them by early Spaniards who heard them called *Apachu,* or Enemy, by the Zunis.

Having achieved warrior status in this society, Gokhlaye set his sights on a young woman named Alope, and he went to her father, No-po-so, to try to arrange for their marriage. No-po-so asked a high price of many ponies for his daughter's hand, but, undaunted, Gokhlaye came up with the price. He and Alope established their own home and eventually had three children.

In the summer of 1858, the Bedonkohes went south into Mexico to trade. On their way through Sonora towards the destination of Casa Grande, they stopped at a place they called Kaskiyeh, camping outside the city for several days. During those days, they traded with the people in town.

Late one afternoon, returning to their camp, Gokhlaye and others who had been in town with him were met by some of the women from the camp. While they had been absent from the camp, the women said, Mexican soldiers had attacked, killing men, women, and children. They had stolen all the horses and arms and had destroyed the camp and supplies.

The Apaches hid for the rest of the day, then carefully sneaked back into their camp after dark. To his horror, Gokhlaye discovered there that his mother, wife, and three children were among the dead. Only eighty warriors were left alive, and they were almost without weapons and ammunition. Mangas Colorado decided that revenge would have to be postponed. They returned, in mourning, to their homes in Arizona Territory. Gokhlaye grieved deeply and vowed revenge upon all of Mexico.

When the Bedonkohes were finally ready to go back to Mexico for their vengeance, Gokhlaye was appointed to visit the other Apache bands to seek their assistance. He went to the Chokonen, or Chiricahuas, where he spoke with Cochise. "If I am killed," he said, "no one need mourn for me. My people have all been killed in that country, and I, too, will die, if need be."

Cochise and his people agreed to join the Bedonkohes on their mission, and Gokhlaye went next to the Nedni Apaches. There he talked with the influential Whoa (or Juh), and he was again successful.

In the summer of 1859, warriors of the three bands assembled on the Mexican border. They went into Mexico on foot, wearing only moccasins, loin cloths, and bands tied around their foreheads.

Each warrior carried three days' rations. They traveled south through Sonora, going as far as forty miles a day.

When they camped near Kaskiyeh, eight men from the town came out to parley, and the Apaches killed them, expecting this act to draw troops out from the town. They were right. The next day, troops did come out to attack, but they seemed not to have anticipated the size or determination of the Apache force. It was a day of small skirmishes with no clear outcome, but the Apaches did capture the Mexicans' supply train.

Anticipating a big battle the next day, and because they knew that Gokhlaye, among them, had lost the most to the Mexicans and had the most need for revenge, the Apaches gave him the honor of directing the coming fight.

On the second day, the Mexicans attacked with full force, two companies of cavalry and two of infantry, and a full-scale battle raged for about two hours. The Apaches were victorious, and Gokhlaye was prominent in the fighting. Because of the ferocity of the fight, he was given a new name by the Mexicans, the name by which he is still known today: Geronimo.

The rest of the Apaches were satisfied with their revenge following the Battle of Kaskiyeh, but not Geronimo. He made several small raids into Mexico, with only one or two companions along. Then in the summer of 1860, he was able to raise a force of twenty-five warriors. They ambushed and wiped out a company of Mexican cavalry, but because the Apache losses were heavy, it was not considered much of a victory. Geronimo himself was wounded in this fight when a Mexican soldier knocked him unconscious with a blow from the butt of his rifle.

The following summer, Geronimo went again into Mexico, this time with twelve warriors. They captured a pack train of mules and headed home with it, but they were surprised by a troop of Mexican cavalry. Geronimo was twice wounded, once by a shot that grazed his head, and the other a flesh wound to his side. The surprise attack routed the Apaches. They escaped individually, meeting later at a predetermined rendezvous point, to return home empty-handed and unsuccessful. Geronimo was blamed by the People for this failure.

Then three companies of Mexican troops crossed the border, located Geronimo's village and surrounded it under cover of darkness. At daybreak they attacked. There were only about twenty warriors in the village, and Geronimo was still recuperating from his wounds. The Mexicans killed a few warriors and many women and children. The villagers fled for their lives into the hills, and the Mexican soldiers destroyed the village and the supplies, departing for home with four captured Apache women.

But the Bedonkohes survived to raid again into Mexico, and this pattern would be repeated again and again throughout almost the rest of the century. In the meantime, another enemy was quietly encroaching into the territory and lives of the Apaches.

Geronimo had seen his first white men in 1858. They had been surveyors, and in the company of a few other warriors, Geronimo had visited and traded with them. They seemed to get along well enough. Soldiers followed, and a military post was established.

Then, in 1861, Lieutenant George N. Bascom had word sent to Cochise that he wanted to talk to him. Cochise thought nothing wrong and went to Apache Pass, accompanied by five members of his family. When they arrived, they were escorted into a military tent, where Bascom accused Cochise of having kidnapped a white boy and stolen some livestock.

Cochise knew the boy, the son of an Indian woman and a white man named Ward. Ward had beaten the boy, and the boy had fled to Cochise for protection. Bascom would listen to no explanations. He placed Cochise and the others under arrest, but Cochise drew his knife and sliced a hole in the back wall of the tent. Jumping through the hole, he fled, but the others were not able to get out.

In an effort to free his relatives, Cochise captured some white men and offered to exchange prisoners. Bascom refused, and the white captives were killed. Bascom retaliated by hanging Cochise's relatives, and the war was on. Mangas Colorado, seventy years old, and the Bedonkohes, joined with Cochise and the Chiricahuas.

In 1862, General James Carleton led his "California Column" into Apache country. He planned a campaign of extermination against the Apaches and the Navajos, and decided to begin with the Mescalero Apaches. Kit Carson, aware of the general's plan, managed to convince some of the Mescaleros that they should go to Carleton and negotiate a peace before he had time to put his plan into action.

But Carson's plan backfired when two of the Mescalero chiefs he had convinced, along with their escorts, were slaughtered along the way by some of Carleton's command. The soldiers had met them and pretended friendship. They had given them flour and other goods, and then they had gotten them drunk with whiskey. That done, the soldiers had simply murdered the defenseless Mescaleros.

Three other chiefs, Cadette, Chato, and Estrella, did reach Carleton at Santa Fe. They assured him that they were at peace with the white men and only wanted to be left alone. Carleton replied that the only way they could have peace was to leave their country and move to the reservation he had laid out for them at the Bosque Redondo on the Pecos River, watched over by the soldiers at Fort Sumner. These Apaches reluctantly agreed and made the move.

But Mangas Colorado and Cochise fought on. At the Battle of Apache Pass, perhaps as many as 500 Apache warriors ambushed a column of 300 soldiers. Though outnumbered, the soldiers held their own, by the use of large artillery pieces, which the Apaches had not encountered before. And Mangas Colorado was shot in the chest during the fight.

The following year, word was sent to Mangas Colorado that the soldiers wanted to talk peace.

Old, weakened from his wound, and facing larger numbers of soldiers and newer weapons, he decided that he should at least go and talk.

The old chief went alone into the army camp, feeling safe because the soldiers were flying a flag of truce. Two guards were placed with him for the night, and the general in charge, Joseph West, told the guards, "I want him dead or alive tomorrow morning." West paused, and lowered his voice. "Do you understand? I want him dead."

The two guards and the old chief sat around a small fire in the dark of the night, and the soldiers heated their bayonets in the fire and touched them to his legs and feet. When at last he jumped up to protest, they shot him. The army report explained that Mangas Colorado had been killed, trying to escape.

Then Cochise mounted a campaign designed to drive all white people out of Apache country. Assisted by the leadership of Victorio and Nana, he kept up a relentless warfare for the next two years. In April of 1865, the United States again made overtures of peace, and Victorio and Nana went into Santa Rita to meet with a government representative. The two chiefs were ready to make peace, but the agent told them that they could only achieve it by removing to the Bosque Redondo. They asked for some time to think it over. Some went to Mexico. Others joined with Cochise.

Five more years of warfare followed. Then in 1871, the United States government set aside four reservations in New Mexico and Arizona for the various bands of Apaches. The government was eagerly trying to contact Cochise. He was seen as the key to it all, and they wanted to get him to visit Washington to negotiate a treaty.

It was during the spring of 1871 that Eskiminzin, chief of a small band of Aravaipa Apaches, went into Camp Grant to talk to Lieutenant Royal E. Whitman. Eskiminzin and his people wanted only to live in peace. He asked to sign a treaty with the United States that would allow him and his people to continue their peaceful lives on the land where they lived.

Whitman asked Eskiminzin why he didn't simply move to the reservation. Eskiminzin's answer was that his people could not make a living there. Lacking the authority to negotiate any further, Whitman told Eskiminzin to camp near the fort until he could receive instructions from his superiors. Eskiminzin and his people did as Whitman suggested.

Then the Indians were attacked by a band of vigilantes from Tucson and nearly wiped out. Investigating the scene, Whitman found one hundred bodies. One was that of an old man, and one was an adolescent boy. The rest were women and children. Further discoveries brought the total dead to 144.

Cochise heard of this, and he could not be convinced to trust the white people. He himself had once been arrested under a flag of truce. Mangas Colorado had been murdered under one, and now, supposedly under the protection of the United States Army, Eskiminzin and the Aravaipas had been subjected to a brutal and murderous attack.

The savagery of the slaughter at Camp Grant did bring the Apache wars to national attention, and President Ulysses S. Grant ordered the United States Army and the Indian Bureau to take some kind of decisive action to bring about peace with the Apaches. He assigned General George Crook to the territory. In addition, Vincent Colyer was sent as a special representative of the Indian Bureau.

Colyer managed to contact Eskiminzin and Delshay, leader of yet another band of Apaches, and to reach agreements with both. But Crook wanted Cochise for himself. He ordered out five companies of cavalry to search out the famous chief, but Cochise had crossed into Mexico. Then Cochise sent word to General Gordon Granger at Santa Fe that he would meet with him at Canada Alamosa to talk peace.

Other Apache leaders were giving up. The United States Army was getting bigger and was better armed all the time. More and more white people were moving into the territory, and Cochise was almost sixty years old. It was time.

Following negotiations with Granger, Cochise agreed to live at peace on a reservation at Canada Alamosa, but after only a few months, the government ordered the removal of all Apaches to the reservation at Tularosa. Cochise and his people fled again.

President Grant sent General O. O. Howard to make peace with Cochise. Howard took with him Tom Jeffords, a white man who was an old friend of Cochise. After an eleven-day conference, a peace satisfactory to both sides was concluded, and Howard had Jeffords appointed agent for the new reservation.

But the troubles were not over. Delshay had agreed with Colyer to make peace and settle at a reservation in Sunflower Valley, but he was not contacted again and received no treaty to sign. He decided that he was still a free Apache and could roam at will. The white people did not agree, and soldiers were sent out after him.

They caught up with him in April of 1873, and their overwhelming numbers forced him to surrender. He and his Tonto Apaches were settled on the White Mountain Reservation, where they were forced to wear dog tags around their necks and could not leave without a written permit.

After a few months of this, Delshay led his people in a flight to the reservation at Rio Verde, where a civilian agent was in charge, and the agent said that they could stay.

Then there was a small uprising at San Carlos, and a soldier was killed. The men involved fled to Rio Verde. Crook accused Delshay of aiding the fugitives and put a price on his head. Two different Apache scouts brought in heads, and Crook paid them both.

At the same time, Crook, in one of his last acts before being transferred north to fight the Sioux and Cheyenne, ordered Eskiminzin arrested simply because he was a chief. Eskiminzin and his Aravaipas were settled back at Camp Grant and were doing well. They'd had nothing to do with the business at San Carlos.

Eskiminzin escaped from confinement in January of 1874 and led his people into the mountains, but they could not find sufficient food and shelter. Cold, hungry, and sick, they went to San Carlos to surrender. The old chief was put in chains. That same year, Cochise died.

The various bands of Apaches were moved and moved again because of government efforts to consolidate them, and, by 1875, they were all confined on reservations, all but those who had fled to Mexico.

One of the leaders of those who crossed the border (rather than be taken to San Carlos as part of the consolidation effort), was Geronimo, now forty-six years old. Because of his long alliance with Cochise, the Bedonkohe Apache by this time considered himself a Chiricahua. In Mexico, Geronimo continued his practice of attacking Mexicans. From time to time, members of Geronimo's band slipped back across the border to visit friends and relatives on the reservations.

In 1877, Agent John Clum (who later founded the *Tombstone Epitaph*) was ordered to round up the Apaches at Ojo Caliente and resettle them at San Carlos. At the same time, he was to arrest any "renegades" found in the area. Two companies of scouts were sent down from San Carlos, and word was passed along to Geronimo and Victorio to come in for a talk. When they did, they were arrested, and Geronimo was put in irons and confined to the guardhouse. He was kept prisoner for four months and transferred to San Carlos.

Clum had established Apache police at San Carlos and believed that he could work with the

Apaches to police themselves and keep them peaceful on the reservation, but the army, because of the concentration of leaders there, sent the cavalry in to guard the reservation. Clum resigned in protest.

Conditions at San Carlos worsened. Rations were short, and people who could not walk into the agency for their rations simply received none. Victorio and his Warm Springs band moved back to Ojo Caliente. Then followed nearly two years of sporadic fighting and negotiations, after which Victorio at last fled into Mexico with eighty warriors, vowing war against the United States forever. He was killed in 1880 in a fight with Mexican soldiers.

Nana, who was seventy years old, escaped from the fight and built up his own guerrilla band. He led a remarkable raid up into Arizona Territory in the summer of 1881, killing and burning everything in his path and recrossing the border with many stolen horses.

At San Carlos, more cavalry was brought in, and rumors began to circulate that all Apache leaders would be arrested. More specifically, the rumors said that Geronimo was to be hanged. In September of 1881, in response to these rumors, Geronimo, Whoa, and about seventy Chiricahua warriors fled the reservation and rode across the border into Mexico.

Six months later, they returned to the reservation in an attempt to persuade others to join them. They got most of the Chiricahua and Warm Springs Apaches to agree and, once again, headed for Mexico. Near the border, pursuing cavalry caught up with them. The warriors fought a rear-guard action, allowing the women and children to get across the border, but then Mexican troops attacked from the other side.

Most of the women and children were slaughtered. Chato, Geronimo, and two other leaders escaped to join up with old Nana.

In 1882, General Crook was returned to command at San Carlos, and, for some reason, he seems to have undergone a profound change. This time, he talked with Apaches on the reservation, and he became convinced that their grievances were real and that they had just cause to distrust the United States Government and white men. He began conducting investigations into the corrupt practices of white contractors and suppliers and set about instituting reforms, including reestablishing the Apache police first created by John Clum.

Crook did not want another war with the Apaches, and he decided that the best place to meet with Geronimo and the other leaders was in Mexico. But in order to cross the border, he had to wait for the Apaches to make a raid in the United States. By international agreement, he could go into Mexico only in pursuit of "hostile" Apaches.

At last, in 1883, Chato led a raid on a mining camp near Tombstone. It was the excuse Crook needed, and he took a force of fifty soldiers and civilian interpreters and 200 Apache scouts across the border. After searching for several weeks, the scouts located Geronimo's camp, but Geronimo and the warriors were out on a raid.

But Crook did manage to meet with Geronimo

and to have lengthy talks. When Crook agreed that Geronimo and the others had probably been treated badly at San Carlos, and when he said that he did not intend to take away their weapons, Geronimo agreed to return, but, he said, it would take him several months to gather up all the Chiricahuas. Crook took him at his word and went back to San Carlos to wait. A large number of the Apaches returned to San Carlos in May. Geronimo and the rest arrived in February of 1884.

Things were peaceful for another year on the reservation, but the white citizens of the Arizona Territory stirred up trouble once again. Newspapers contained stories about Geronimo, accusing him of all sorts of depredations and calling him an inhuman monster. Some suggested that Crook had surrendered to Geronimo in Mexico. Others called on vigilante action to hang Geronimo if the army would not do it.

These tales reached Geronimo's ears, and in May of 1885, he, old Nana, another Apache named Chihuahua, and Mangas, the son of Mangas Colorado, decided to go to Mexico. Geronimo asked Chato to go with them, but Chato refused. Geronimo, with ninety-two women and children, and thirty-four men, after cutting the telegraph wire, left the reservation.

Chihuahua changed his mind along the way and dropped out with his band. They were going back. A pursuing column of cavalry met them along the way and attacked them, before they could explain. Furious, Chihuahua led a series of vicious retaliatory raids, for which Geronimo received the blame.

GERONIMO

Geronimo, in the meantime, was doing his best to avoid any contact with white people. He just wanted to get across the border, and he did. Crook knew then that he would have to return to Mexico in order to deal with Geronimo, and that was the beginning of the campaign of 1886.

Chapter 1

It was dawn in the Sierra Madre of Mexico. A small band of Chiricahua Apaches were making their way across an open flat. The Chiricahuas were the last of the great tribes to defy the United States government in its effort to impose the reservation system on all Indians.

Some few warriors were mounted, but most of the people were on foot. The majority were women and children. Off to their right, a rocky hillside rose up from the desert floor. The Apaches moved at an angle, headed for the rocks. To their left, across the flat, was a gully.

In the gully were hidden two companies of the United States Sixth Cavalry, dismounted, waiting in tense silence. The Sixth, under the command of Brigadier General George Crook, was entrusted with the responsibility of breaking the resistance of the Chiricahuas.

On the gully's rim, Crook himself lay, looking at the Apaches through a pair of field glasses. Beside him was Al Sieber, his chief of scouts.

Crook lowered the glasses but continued to stare ahead at the Apaches across the flat.

"Geronimo?" he asked, handing the glasses to Sieber. The scout took them and raised them to his eyes.

"He won't be here," Sieber said. "This is the rear guard. They'll fight a delaying action. Twenty-five, maybe thirty warriors. Maybe a hundred women and children."

He lowered the glasses and handed them back to the general.

"The warriors will turn and fight," said Crook. "There's no avoiding it. That would give the women and children time to make it to cover."

"One thing's for damn sure," said Sieber. "They already know we're here."

Crook turned his head to look down the gully at the anxious troopers waiting there.

"Captain Ragsdale," he called.

"Sir," snapped the captain in response.

"Troopers on the flat," ordered Crook. "Form a line."

"Sir," said Ragsdale. He turned his head to look down the line in the wash and called out in a loud and clear voice, "A and B Companies, forward, march."

The soldiers led their mounts up out of the wash and formed a line as Crook and Sieber moved toward them. A trooper came out to them leading their mounts, Sieber's horse and Crook's big army mule. Crook swung up into the saddle, as did Sieber, and Ragsdale mounted up the troops.

"Al," said Crook, "scouts to the left flank."

"Yessir," said Sieber, turning his mount. Then he yelled, "Scouts."

As Sieber rode off to the left followed by armed Apache scouts, Crook moved over next to Captain Ragsdale.

"Captain Ragsdale," he said.

"Sir."

"Advance carbines."

"Company," called Ragsdale. "Advance carbines."

All down the line, troopers responded to the order, as Crook and Ragsdale pulled out their revolvers.

"Sound the march," said Crook.

"Bugler," called Ragsdale.

The sudden, unmistakable, brass sound of the cavalry charge blared in the dry desert air. It carried across the flat to the ears of the fleeing Apaches, who heard the notes and read them accurately. They had heard them often enough before.

Women, children, and old men ran for the imagined safety of the rocks. Warriors, armed with rifles, some mounted, some on foot, shouted, urging them on, as those on horseback moved themselves to positions between those on foot and the charging soldiers.

With the full cavalry charge coming toward them, the mounted Apaches, not waiting for the onslaught, raised their rifles and raced forward in a countercharge to meet the enemy head on. If they could engage the White-eyes halfway across the flat, the others would have more time to reach the shelter of the rocks. It was, as Sieber had correctly surmised, a calculated delaying action.

Then the soldiers began to fire, reloading at the gallop. An Apache horse fell, tossing its rider into the air, and close by, a warrior was knocked from his horse when a soldier's bullet smashed into his chest. The earlier silence of the desert had been shattered by the deadly sounds of sudden battle: gunshots, shouts, screams of men and horses, the pounding of hoofs.

Most of the women and children reached the rocks and began their desperate climb. The warriors on foot stood below the rocks urging them on, firing occasionally at the troopers to aid their mounted companions. Then the horseback warriors turned and rode back to join them there at the base of the outcropping of rocks, and all the Apache warriors quickly formed a skirmish line, firing rapidly at the charging cavalry.

It was a battle typical of the many battles fought between the Chiricahua Apaches and the United States Army, and it ended typically, with dead on both sides and the army holding a handful of captives, mostly women and children. The remaining Apaches had fled into the obscurity of the rocky hills to be pursued once more.

Crook rode alone, far ahead of the two seasoned companies of Sixth Cavalry that followed him.

Behind him, the long dusty column of blue-uniformed soldiers was headed up by twenty Apache scouts and trailed by a pack train of mules. But Crook rode well ahead of the rest. He was not a fool. Farther out in front, well beyond his vision, were his most trusted scouts: Chato and Sergeant Turkey, both Apaches, and the white Chief of Scouts, Al Sieber. With a handful of other Apache scouts and under the command of Captain Hentig, they would get the job done. They had their orders, and they knew what they were doing.

Crook rode a big army mule. He favored mules over horses for military campaigns. He wore khaki trousers held up by wide galluses, and a light canvas jacket. His short-cropped hair was mostly covered by his cork sun helmet, but his full, forked beard, liberally sprinkled with gray, bristled. He carried a shotgun across his saddle, another of the many eccentricities for which he was widely known. He rode easy, but his eyes were alert to his surroundings.

It was dawn, and the sun coming up over the Mexican desert was already bright in the sky. Crook knew that the day would grow hot. Beyond the dry hills ahead, he could see black smoke billowing up into the sky, and he knew what waited for him over there for he was the man who had set it all in motion. Whatever was happening or had already happened was his own personal responsibility. Any glory or any shame that resulted from this day would be his and his alone. He knew that, and he accepted it. And then he heard the shots.

On the other side of the low dry hills, what had

only recently been a Chiricahua Apache village of hastily constructed, dome-shaped, brush-covered wickieups was mostly in flames. Women shouted in shrill voices and rushed to protect their children from the sudden attack. Old men fought desperately. Children screamed and cried, and dogs barked.

An Apache scout came running out of a wickieup with stolen booty in his hands. Once he was safely outside, another Apache scout stuck a torch to the dry dwelling place, and the crackling flames leaped high, thickening the already smoke-filled air.

An old Chiricahua man came stumbling out of the flaming wickieup, an ancient cap and ball revolver in his hand. Two of the scouts, Chato and Sergeant Turkey, raised their own military-issue Colt single-action .45 revolvers almost simultaneously and fired. The old man jerked twice and fell forward to die in front of his burning home.

General George Crook topped the rise, leading the rest of the troops. He sat for a moment in the saddle taking in the scene below. These Apache scouts were efficient. In fact, he well knew, the only way to fight Apaches was to enlist other Apaches to help get the job done. He was the man who had made that discovery and initiated the practice. He urged his mule forward and rode into the midst of the carnage and confusion.

A small Apache child, a little girl, stood bewildered, trembling, looking up at the stolid face of the Apache scout Chato. Captain Hentig, in charge of the attack force, walked over to stand beside Chato. He tried not to look at the child. Hentig was forty-five years old, a product of West Point. At the

Point he had not been taught about making war on women and children, and his years of experience since had not taught him to like it. It was ugly, distasteful work. Hentig longed for a battlefield where two opposing armies would meet to fight, with no civilians anywhere near.

"Where's Geronimo and all the warriors?" he asked the scout, almost accusingly. "There's no one here but women and children. A few old men. I thought you said this was Geronimo's camp."

"All gone to raid," said Chato. Neither his face nor his voice betrayed any sign of emotion. "This is Geronimo's camp."

Crook rode his mule over to where Hentig and Chato were standing. The fight, if it could be called such, was over. Bodies were lying around in grotesque positions. A small group of women and children huddled together, surrounded by Apache scouts pointing guns at them. The children cried. Women held them close. Off to one side of the village, another group of scouts gathered Apache horses together. Hentig gave the general a smart salute, and Crook acknowledged it casually, almost sloppily.

"Sir," said Hentig, "we've secured the mustangs." He gestured toward the small herd. "It looks like most of them have been stolen from ranches here in Mexico."

Crook seemed not to hear what his captain had said. He looked down at the little girl who was still staring, still bewildered, still trembling with fear. "Is she hurt?" he asked. "Get someone over here. Get the surgeon."

As Hentig ran to obey the command, Crook swung down out of the saddle. He leaned over to pick up the child, and when he did, she began to cry out loud and to shake more violently than before. He might as well have been some horrible, shaggy monster, and in the eyes of the little Apache girl, he supposed that he was just that. He tried to hold her close, her head down on his shoulder, and he patted her gently on the back.

"It'll be all right," he said, attempting to make his voice as soothing as possible. "I swear it will. It'll get better."

He looked out over the scene again, at the bodies lying around, at the flames, at the Apache scouts collecting and dividing up among themselves the spoils of war, and he held the child tightly against his shoulder, trying desperately to give her some comfort. He felt tears sting his eyes, and he fought them back.

Al Sieber walked over to take a look at the tethered Apache horses. Fifty years old with dark hair beginning to gray and a drooping mustache, Sieber was a white man, a civilian employed by the United States Army as Chief of Scouts. A veteran, he was known as an expert tracker, and he could speak the Apache language.

The horses were being watched over and admired by some of the Apache scouts who had gathered them together. A couple of them still ran loose, and the Apaches were chasing after them. Sieber looked quickly over the herd, but he found himself particularly interested in one big black stallion.

"Some of these are damn fine animals," he said.

The black stallion ran loose, but the scouts ran in front of him waving their arms and shouting. Amid the confusion and general chaos as the scouts attempted to control him, the horse ran in circles, loudly neighing with fright. Sieber watched the animal for a moment.

"Look at that," he said. "Look at him prance. Old Geronimo must have stole him off some real big rich ranchero. That stallion's got some fine bloodstock in him. Yes, sir!"

He studied the stallion, fascinated with the animal's movements, then waved an arm toward a couple of scouts who stood nearby looking on.

"Somebody get a rope on him," he said. "Pronto. I don't want him to break a leg or something."

Back in the village, by this time reduced to ashes, the old men, women, and children who had survived the attack stood herded tightly together. Among them was an old warrior known and recognized by Crook and Sieber. He was old Nana. The captives were still surrounded by Apache scouts who still held rifles and revolvers, cocked and ready to fire, as if they feared that these helpless ones might yet decide to counterattack. The faces of the captives all registered fear and hate.

Crook walked over to stand beside Chato. He had given the little girl over to the surgeon.

"Tell old Nana and the others we won't hurt them," he said. "Then pick out two of the women to carry a message for us. Get them a couple of good horses and some food."

While Chato spoke to them in Apache, Al Sieber moved up to stand beside Crook. Chato finished what he was saying and gave Crook a glance.

"Tell them to go find their men," said the general. "Tell them we're not going anywhere. We don't want to fight. We are here to take them to a reservation. Tell them to tell their men that Nantan Lupan only wants peace with the Chiricahua."

Again Chato repeated, in Apache, what Crook had said. Crook, finished, walked away. He headed for a pack mule which stood close by. Captain Hentig stood watching Chato, and Al Sieber stepped over to stand beside him.

Crook changed his jacket and picked up an ammo belt and a Parker 12-gauge shotgun. He walked back over to Sieber's side and stood for a moment, staring off into the distance. "He's out there," he said. "Somewhere."

"Geronimo?" said Sieber. "Yep. He's out there all right. I'd say close."

"I'm going hunting," said Crook, and he turned abruptly to walk away.

Chapter 2

Britton Davis was twenty-two years old, a West Point graduate, anticipating his first assignment to garrison life. Suffering the rough stagecoach ride into Arizona Territory in the early summer of 1885, he was preoccupied with conflicting emotions. He was a stranger to the Great American Desert, and he himself was as yet untried as a soldier. He wondered what military life would be like, and how he would fare. Of course, he fully intended to acquit himself well. He hoped that he would. He had planned for a military career, and he wasn't about to jeopardize it on his first assignment. He felt himself full of hopes, dreams, uncertainties, and anxieties.

As a West Point cadet, he had been filled with tales of glory and honor. He had been taught, and he firmly believed, that the United States of America was the greatest experiment in democracy the world had ever known, and it was to be his own personal honor to serve in its military in the great cause of freedom and liberty and justice. And he believed fervently in those ideals. He had sworn that he would fight and die, if necessary, to uphold them. In short, Britton Davis had the heart and soul of a true patriot.

But rolling across the desert in a stagecoach, it was difficult to keep his ideals in mind. He felt tired and worn, as if someone had been beating him with a stick all over his body. The stagecoach constantly rocked and jerked violently, tossing him and the other passengers back and forth, slamming them against the back wall or the sides, and occasionally into each other. It was impossible to rest or relax, and sleeping was totally out of the question.

At night, his teeth had chattered from the cold, and in the heat of the day, his military uniform was soaked with perspiration. And he was caked with the dust of the desert. He longed for a hot bath and a soft bed, and, after that, a clean uniform to wear. He also longed for human companionship, for the other passengers had all disembarked at earlier stops along the way. Since riding into the hot desert, Davis had been alone inside the stage.

Then over the general clatter of the stagecoach and the pounding of hoofs, Davis heard the loud, raspy shout of Buck the driver, and felt the coach lurch and turn. He leaned over to look out the window, and he saw that they were approaching a low adobe building beside a corral. Both structures appeared to be standing, except for the company of each other, in the middle of nowhere.

As they drew closer, Davis saw a Mexican boy in front of the adobe jump up and shout. Three vaqueros came out of the small structure to await the arrival of the coach. Buck yelled again, and again Davis felt the coach veer. He could see that they were moving through a gate into the station yard, and he marveled at the skill of the driver. They did not seem to have slowed much, yet they raced through the gate and on toward the small house.

Then they came to a sudden stop in front of the station, and the coach gave a violent lurch forward, then back, then settled down to a steady rocking motion. Davis heard Buck talking loudly, presumably to the vaqueros—and to the horses.

"Be careful of old Molly now," he was saying. "Take it easy. Hold it steady there, girl. That's it. That's the way. Steady now."

Davis saw Curly, riding shotgun, climb down. Buck was getting off on the other side. Davis opened the door, grabbed his hatbox, and stepped out onto solid ground. He stretched and twisted, trying to get the kinks out of his much-abused body. The vaqueros were busy changing the horses on the stage. A middle-aged white man, dressed in dirty clothes and needing a shave and a hair cut, stood waiting about halfway between the coach and the station house. As Davis looked up at his face, the man scratched his belly and grinned broadly, showing bad teeth.

"Howdy," he said. "I'm Billy Pickett, station manager."

"Second Lieutenant Britton Davis, United States Army," said Davis. "Pleased to meet you, sir."

"Welcome," said Pickett. "It always does me good to see an army fellow out here."

Davis's suitcase landed beside him with a thud, sending up a cloud of dry desert dust. Davis looked around at the vast, desolate expanse, and he found the sight almost overwhelming, but he had another, more practical reaction to the emptiness around him. It was something akin to panic brought about by a fear of abandonment. He tried to shrug it off.

"Is there no one here to meet me, sir?" he asked Pickett.

"Nope," said Pickett. "Not a soul. Who was you expecting?"

"I guess—someone from the Sixth Cavalry," said Davis, and he was all of a sudden feeling a little unsure of himself.

"Looks like they forgot you was coming," said Pickett, with a grin. "Or more likely, they got some kind of Apache trouble. Hell, don't worry about it. Someone'll come along sooner or later, I reckon. You come on inside, and get yourself something to eat."

Davis picked up his battered and dusty suitcase and followed Pickett into the low adobe station. There was nothing else for him to do, and he was hungry. In a short time, he found himself seated alone at a long dust-covered table. Everything in the station seemed to be covered with a permanent layer of dust. A tin plate of beans and bread was there on the table in front of him. He ate greedily. Across the room was a stand-up bar. After having served Davis his food, Pickett had moved on over behind the bar.

"Whiskey?" asked the station manager, holding up a half-empty bottle of brown liquid.

Davis swallowed a mouthful of beans.

"No, thank you, sir," he said.

"You don't have to 'sir' me, son," said Pickett. "I ain't no officer."

He put a glass on the bar and poured himself a drink, which he tossed off at once. "Ah," he said. "That's damn good stuff." Then he poured another. "Where you from, Lieutenant?" he asked.

"I was born in Texas," said Davis, "near Brownsville."

"Texas? Well, hell, son, I thought you was from somewhere back east. You kind of got that manner about you, you know."

Davis smiled a bit self-consciously. His mind wasn't really on this conversation. He was worrying about what he would do if no one showed up to escort him to his new post.

"Well," he said, "I've been the last four years at West Point."

The door opened and a vaquero stuck his head inside.

"Señor," he said. *"Soldados vienen."*

Through the open doorway, Davis could hear the sound of horses' hoofs. He stood, grabbed his hatbox, and walked across the room to look out a window. He saw a cavalry officer and what he assumed to be three Apache scouts riding into the station yard. Davis had never seen an Apache, much less an Apache scout, but he had heard of them.

He whipped the soft kepi off his head, opened the hatbox and took out a fine new wide-brimmed cavalry hat. He put it on his head, dropped the kepi in the box, picked up the hatbox in one hand and his suitcase in the other and struggled through the doorway to get outside. The four riders were halting their mounts in front of the building as he stepped out.

"Lieutenant Britton Davis?" asked the mounted officer, whom Davis had by then identified as a first lieutenant.

Davis dropped his suitcase and saluted smartly.

"Yes, sir," he said. "At your service, sir."

The mounted officer returned the salute.

"First Lieutenant Charles B. Gatewood," he said. "General Crook asked me to swing by and pick you up. As a matter of convenience. We're on our way south."

He swung down out of the saddle, and a vaquero hurried up to take his horse and lead it to the water trough which lay nearby. The three Apaches dismounted and followed the vaquero with their own horses. One of them, Davis noticed, was leading a riderless but saddled horse.

"The sorrel being led by Sergeant Chato there is yours," said Gatewood. "We'll have your suitcase sent on over to the fort." He glanced down at the hatbox in Davis's left hand. "And that," he added. "Welcome to Arizona Territory, Lieutenant. We're on our way to bring in Geronimo."

Geronimo. The name sent a thrill through the veins of Davis. He tried very hard to appear calm, even casual, over the surprising news, and he even wondered if the lieutenant might be pulling his leg. Perhaps this was some kind of joke played on fresh officers new to the desert. Geronimo was a name which struck terror into the hearts of people who lived well beyond his reach. Eastern newspapers were full of tales of the horrors of Geronimo. How, he asked himself, could two officers and three Apache scouts be bringing in Geronimo? But he kept all of these thoughts to himself.

"Yes, sir," he said.

"He's due in a few days," said Gatewood. "We'll go on down to the border to meet him and then escort him back to San Carlos. It's seventy-five miles to the border, Mr. Davis. You'll have plenty of time to get acquainted with your new mount."

"Sir?" said Davis.

"Yes?"

"Just you and me? Just the two of us?" He nodded toward the scouts. "And them?"

"The general figured that with Geronimo along, we wouldn't likely need much more in the way of protection," said Gatewood. "What do you think?"

"Yes, sir," said Davis, but he was not able to hide his puzzlement. Gatewood smiled.

"A small detachment," he said, "means that we'll not be seen as threatening by the hostiles. Now you wouldn't want to pose a threat to Geronimo, would you, Mr. Davis?"

"No, sir," said Davis, forcing a smile in return. *Geronimo.* The name had been given to the man, from what Davis had heard, by Mexicans, because of his ferocity. What did it mean? Outcast? Renegade? Something like that. And the three scouts at the water trough were the only Apaches Davis had ever seen. He had only just disembarked in the Arizona Territory, was still marveling at the sight of the Great American Desert, and he was about to ride seventy-five miles across that vast expanse with only one other soldier to meet up with Geronimo, to actually see the famous man, perhaps the most feared man in the world, face to face. He found himself wishing that he had time to write another letter to his mother.

It was noon of the third day of riding across the open desert, and the sun was intense overhead. Davis, Gatewood, and the three Apache scouts, whom Davis had come to know by the names of Chato, Dutchy, and Sergeant Turkey, still moved south across the sandy expanse.

He had learned from Gatewood, in bits and pieces, that Geronimo had, in effect, surrendered to General Crook, and that he had agreed to cross the border from Mexico back into Arizona Territory at a specified time. Gatewood, with Davis along, was on his way to meet Geronimo and escort him to San Carlos. That information made Davis a little less uneasy with his new mission.

During the ride, Davis formed a generally good impression of Gatewood. He was possessed of a military brusqueness, Davis had noted, but it was balanced by unfailing good manners, and he was clearly a man of confidence and of some considerable experience in the Apache wars. And he had a sense of humor. Davis liked that.

"That's the border," said Gatewood, pointing ahead and reining in his mount. He took out a compass and aimed it, pointing to infinity. "Geronimo's out there somewhere—probably fighting Mexicans."

"How will he find us?" asked Davis.

Gatewood snapped his compass shut and put it away.

"Easy," he said. "We're the only ones out here." He swung a leg over the back of his horse and dropped to the ground. The three scouts also dismounted and started to unpack their mules. Davis was the last climb down out of the saddle.

He was stiff and sore. He stood staring ahead toward the Mexican border, and then he saw something move, the figure of a man appearing over a sand dune. He took out his field glasses and saw through them what appeared to be a young Apache man beating a small drum and singing.

"Lieutenant?" he said.

"Apache medicine man," said Gatewood, raising his own glasses to get a better look.

"Out there all alone?" said Davis.

"He's probably on a pilgrimage of some kind," said Gatewood. He looked over his shoulder at the scouts, all three of whom were by then staring at the lone Apache off in the distance. "Apaches believe in their . . . power," Gatewood continued. "It's a kind of spirit they carry around inside them."

Davis stared at the medicine man for another moment in silence, then lowered his glasses to look over at Gatewood. He knew the mission, and he knew what Gatewood had told him about Geronimo's surrender. But standing near the Mexican border with no sign of civilization of any kind anywhere in sight and seeing the Apache appear seemingly out of nowhere, thinking of Geronimo and his ferocious reputation, he suddenly felt very vulnerable with only Gatewood and three Apaches for company.

"Sir?" he said. "Geronimo's just going to come on in and give himself up?"

"That's what he promised," said Gatewood. "A Chiricahua doesn't give his word much, but when he does, he keeps it. As long as you keep yours."

At dusk, the small detachment was camped and still waiting. Gatewood and Davis had pitched a small canvas tent, and a short distance away, a tarp was stretched on poles to make a kind of arbor. A small fire burned between the tent and the tarp, and the medicine man who had earlier been observed from a distance, sat at the fire chanting in a low voice. He had come in earlier and talked to Chato, then made himself at home. Chato had said something to Gatewood about it in Apache, but when Davis had asked for an explanation, Gatewood had only shrugged.

The scouts were under the tarp playing cards. Gatewood and Davis sat inside the tent at a table playing checkers. Davis jumped Gatewood. He glanced out through the open door of the tent to look at the medicine man. Then he looked back at Gatewood.

"You don't talk much to them, do you?"

"To an Apache," said Gatewood, "stillness is a pleasure. They're taught that when they're young. It helps someone who may have to hide and wait."

There was a moment of silence before Davis spoke up again. "What's he singing about?" he asked, nodding his head in the direction of the medicine man.

"He's trying to locate Geronimo," said Gatewood.

Just then Chato walked over to the tent and squatted just outside the doorway.

"Geronimo will be here," he said. "Medicine man says three days. Maybe more."

"Is he riding a horse or a mule?" asked Gatewood, and Davis thought that Gatewood was making a subtle joke at his expense about the supposed powers of the medicine man. He often had the feeling that Gatewood and the scouts were saying things only for his benefit, trying to amaze him or frighten him because he was new to the territory. It was kind of like an initiation process. The only problem with it was that Davis couldn't tell when they were telling the truth and when they were pulling his leg. But then, he told himself, that's the whole point of that kind of joking, isn't it?

"Caballo blanco," said Chato. He glanced at Davis and added, "A white horse."

Gatewood looked at Davis as Chato stood up and walked back toward the other scouts under the tarp. "Five dollars says Geronimo rides in here on a white horse," he said.

Davis smirked a little. He wasn't quite sure yet

about Gatewood's brand of humor, but Gatewood had left himself open on this one. He'd made the offer based on his own joke. It seemed to Davis to be a sure thing. Well, he was tired of being the butt of all the jokes. He'd take Gatewood's five dollars and enjoy spending it, if he ever again found himself someplace where he could spend money.

"Just because the medicine man said it? You've got a bet, Lieutenant," he said. He pushed back his chair and stood up. Moving to the doorway, he squatted down to look out toward the card players across the way.

"Question," he said. "These scouts we have with us, they're Apaches, right? Why would they work for the army? Why do they fight against their own kind?"

"Are you asking if we can trust them, Mr. Davis?" said Gatewood.

"Well, yes, sir, I suppose I am," said Davis. "Or at least, I guess I'm asking *why* we can trust them."

"Oh, well," said Gatewood, "there are lots of different reasons, I guess. For one thing, the money's good. And don't think that money doesn't mean anything to an Indian. They've learned what it's good for.

"Then, too, there are several different bands of Apaches, and they don't always get along with each other. Most of all, though, I think, Apaches go where the best fight is. It's a kind of morality with them, once you understand it."

"Is that an advantage?" asked Davis.

"It's how we beat them," said Gatewood. He

leaned forward to look out the door, and then he gave a shout.

"Chato," he called. The scout turned to look toward the tent. "Chato, tell Mr. Davis here how many raids did you lead against the White-eyes."

"Many," said Chato. "For many years, I raid across the border."

Gatewood turned his attention back to Davis. "Now, Chato's our best scout," he said. "And most loyal. Right, Chato?" He raised his voice again with the last two words, and Chato looked back, questioningly. "You're the most loyal scout," Gatewood repeated in a loud voice. "Right?"

Chato's reply was a mere nod of the head. Davis stared at the scout for a moment, then stood up to go back to his chair. His legs were numb and tingling from the overlong squat. He sat back down across the table from Gatewood and stretched out his legs.

So, he thought, Chato had fought against the United States Army, and now he was the army's most loyal scout. It didn't make any sense to Davis, even after all that Gatewood had said, but he decided that he had already asked too many questions. He noticed that Gatewood had reset the checkerboard.

"It's your move, Lieutenant," said Gatewood.

Davis sat back down and looked at the board. He sighed and moved a piece. Gatewood jumped it. It looked like it was going to be a long, hot, boring two or three days.

Chapter 3

The late-afternoon sun blazed down with what seemed to Lieutenant Davis to be a new and deliberately hostile intensity. He sat again with Gatewood in the tent, its sides rolled up because of the sweltering heat. They no longer played checkers. They had switched to poker, using bullets for chips. There was really not much else to do while they waited: two officers of the United States Army, three Apache scouts, and one medicine man, all sitting and waiting in a great emptiness for the great Chiricahua warrior, Geronimo.

Davis found himself looking forward to the meeting with mixed and confused emotions. He wondered what Geronimo would be like. He wondered what would happen. Would the fearsome Apache warrior actually just meet them and ride along with them into San Carlos? Would he come with a force and attack them? If so, Davis figured, they wouldn't stand a chance. He kept telling himself that Gatewood seemed to know what he was doing.

"Lieutenant," he said, "just curious. If you don't mind. Are you a family man?"

"Yes, I am," said Gatewood. "I have a son and a daughter with my wife back home in Virginia."

"You must miss them," said Davis.

"I do. Very much," said Gatewood, and his voice suddenly had a lonesome and faraway sound to it. "I miss them every hour of every day."

Gatewood put down his cards, as Davis noticed out of the corner of his eye, Chato walking toward the tent. He hadn't yet quite gotten used to the dark skin and almost black eyes, didn't know if he really trusted the man. What was the difference, he asked himself, between this Apache and that other one, the one for whom they waited, the one for whom the world seemed to have come to a halt out in the middle of nowhere? Was one Apache like another? The scout reached the doorway and squatted. Leaning back in his chair, Davis yawned and stretched, trying to appear casual, trying not to show his curiosity, his mistrust, his—fear? Gatewood studied his cards.

"Chiricahuas here," said Chato. "Geronimo rides a white horse."

The two officers got up quickly and looked outside. Off in the southern distance they could see the hazy image of four armed and mounted

Apaches. Silhouetted against the bright sky and covered in fine alkali dust, they appeared to Davis to be almost ghostlike. He felt a sudden chill in spite of the blistering heat.

Gatewood grabbed his military blouse and began pulling it on over his head. "You owe me five dollars, Mr. Davis," he said.

"The medicine man said three days," said Davis. "They're early."

"An officer and a gentleman doesn't evade his debts," said Gatewood, stuffing the tail of his blouse into his trousers. "The bet wasn't about the time involved. It was about the white horse. You still owe me five dollars."

"Yes, sir," said Davis. "I admit it, and I'll pay it as soon as I can."

"There's no rush, Mr. Davis," said Gatewood.

Davis could see, underneath the rolled-up tent walls, Geronimo on his white horse and the other three Apaches ride to the edge of the camp. He wondered how the medicine man had known that the horse would be white. There was probably a simple explanation. Maybe he had come from the same camp. Maybe Geronimo always rode a white horse.

The other three Apaches stopped there at the camp's edge, but Geronimo kept moving, coming slowly toward them. Davis felt like running for a weapon, but he stood still and watched as Geronimo rode on into the camp and came to a stop up close to Chato, staring down at the scout with a hard and sullen expression on his face.

"I heard you were working for the White-eyes," said Geronimo, speaking to Chato in the Apache language. "I did not believe it. Now I know where your heart truly lies."

Davis, of course, did not know what Geronimo said to Chato, but when Geronimo spat contemptuously and urged his horse forward, there was no mistaking the sense of his message to the scout. He remembered his own earlier question to Gatewood. Why do they fight against their own kind?

Gatewood and Davis stepped out of the tent just in time to meet Geronimo as he halted his white horse in front of the doorway. The other Apaches remained back at the edge of the camp where they had stopped a respectful distance away. They remained mounted. Gatewood seized the initiative and spoke to Geronimo.

"First Lieutenant Charles Gatewood," he said, and then he surprised both Davis and Geronimo by switching with seeming ease to the language of the Apaches. "It's good to see the great warrior Geronimo," he said.

"You speak pretty good Apache for a White-eye," said Geronimo, speaking English. He looked toward Davis, and Davis spoke out, standing at attention.

"Second Lieutenant Britton Davis," he said. "Sixth Cavalry."

Geronimo made no response to Davis's introduction, but instead turned his face back toward Gatewood. Davis felt strangely as if he were greatly outranked in the presence of this man. He had not considered that he would feel that way in front of an Apache Indian, even the great Geronimo. But he had not expected to see such dignity, such pride, such—

"You are now under the protection of the United States Army," said Gatewood, speaking English again. "We will escort you to General Crook at San Carlos."

Geronimo made no response, so Gatewood spoke again.

"Nantan Lupan," he said, "waits for you with an open heart."

Davis was first of all impressed that Geronimo spoke good English, but his next feeling was a strong sense of the tremendous irony of two soldiers with only three scouts in the middle of the vast desert actually offering Geronimo their protection. Davis wondered who would protect him and Gatewood should Geronimo decide to change his mind.

He was glad, though, that the feared Apache leader had decided to use English instead of Apache in which to converse with Gatewood. Listening to even the brief conversation in the other language had made him feel unnecessary, almost redundant, like an extra shadow for Gatewood.

Abruptly, Geronimo turned his white horse and rode back to join the other Apaches who still waited patiently for him at the edge of the camp. Davis, of course, had not understood Gatewood's last words to Geronimo, but he did recognize the first two. He had heard them before.

"Lieutenant, sir," he said, "for my education, just what does Nantan Lupan mean?"

"Gray Wolf Chief," said Gatewood. "The Apaches gave the general that name after his first campaign against them. That was back in—"

"Eighteen-seventy-one, sir," said Davis.

Gatewood gave Davis a look which Davis was unable to read. "You know your recent military history well, Mr. Davis," he said.

Davis stared across the space toward Geronimo and the other Apaches. The medicine man had joined them over there and was singing. At the conclusion of his song, he raised his beaded staff, turned, and walked off into the desert alone. Davis wondered where he was going on foot out in this wilderness. For that matter, where had he come from, and why had he made his strange appearance in their camp? If he was a member of Geronimo's band, why was he not going into San Carlos with the others? He wondered how long it would be before he had anything in his head about this country and these people other than questions.

"They are—something," Davis said.

"The Chiricahuas are special people," said Gatewood, "even among the Apaches."

They stopped at a way station at dusk and watched as the attendants there changed the horses on an eastbound stagecoach. Davis was grateful that he was not among its passengers. He wondered if his luggage had made it to San Carlos.

Geronimo thought that it would be nice if the

stagecoach were carrying all the White-eyes back east and out of the lands of the Apaches. He also thought about the times he had stopped the stage-coaches and robbed them, and a part of him longed to ride after this one and stop it.

The station consisted of a couple of line shacks, some corrals, and an adobe stage depot. Dutchy and Sergeant Turkey stood outside in front of the depot and leaned against the wall to watch the stage roll out. Geronimo wondered if something inside them also longed to rob the stage, or if wearing the blue coats had changed them utterly. Were they still Apaches? He wasn't sure. He followed Gatewood and Davis inside, and Mangas and Ulzana, the other two warriors, followed him.

Inside the depot, Geronimo, Mangus, and Ulzana sat at the long table eating. Davis sat alone at a small table across the room writing a letter to his mother. Gatewood stood shaving in front of a mirror that was hanging on the back wall. A Mexican woman was cooking, and Chato stood looking out the front window. The atmosphere in the room was thick and heavy with the odors of cooking meat and beans.

"Two men are coming," said Chato. "One fellow with white hat. He's carrying a shotgun."

Gatewood hurried over to the window to look out. He looked back at Davis, then at Geronimo. Then he moved quickly back to the mirror to wipe the excess soap off his face. Chato stayed at the window. He watched as the two men outside dis-mounted and tied their horses to the hitching rail.

As they approached the door, he turned his head to keep his eyes on them as they came inside.

The big man in the white hat carried a cut down 10-gauge shotgun which he laid across an elbow when he stepped into the station. The other, a small man who looked like a weasel, wore a bowler. The man in the white hat spoke first.

"I'm looking for the officer in charge here," he said, with a sideways glance at Gatewood. "That must be you, huh?"

"Lieutenant Charles Gatewood," answered Gatewood, tossing aside the towel with which he had just wiped his face. "At your service."

The man turned slowly away from Gatewood to give a long hard look at Geronimo, still seated at the table with the other two Apaches. Then he turned back toward Gatewood.

"We heard a rumor that the army might be traveling through these parts with some hostiles," he said. "Especially one hostile in particular."

He looked again at Geronimo through squinty eyes, and the Apache read easily the contempt and the hatred written on the man's face.

"I'm Joe Hawkins," the man continued, and he took his coat by a lapel and held it open to reveal a badge pinned on the vest underneath. "City Marshal of Tombstone. Those Apaches you got over there with you are under arrest. I'm deputizing you two to hold these criminals here for me till morning, when I can get back with a warrant and a posse to help me take them in."

Gatewood picked up his blue tunic from a chair

and pulled it on, then began fastening the brass buttons. He knew about these men and others like them. They were in Tucson and Tombstone and other towns in the Arizona Territory, and they had friends on military posts and in Washington. They were contractors and friends of contractors who profitted from military campaigns against the Indians, and when there was no trouble, they did their best to stir some up. They spread rumors about Apache depredations that kept the citizenry terrorized.

If Geronimo or any other Apache had actually been guilty of half the atrocities blamed on him by these ruthless profiteers, Gatewood would have shot them down himself. Without these greedy opportunists' interference, Gatewood was convinced, the army's job would have been much easier.

"These Apaches are in our custody, sir," Gatewood said.

"The warrant I'm talking about is going to specify murder of white citizens," said Hawkins, raising his voice, "also horse thievery and hostile Indianism. Is that good enough for you, soldier boy?"

Davis stood up and stepped over to stand beside Gatewood. At the same time, Hawkins's weasel-faced deputy stepped forward.

"We mean to do what's right by them," said the deputy, spreading his mouth in a toothy grin, "which in this case means that we intend to hang them."

He laughed, a nervous little laugh. Davis felt a revulsion growing from deep down in his guts. Something in him wanted to hit Weasel Face in the nose.

"My orders," said Gatewood, "are to turn these Apaches over to General Crook."

"And the United States Army doesn't need any help from the likes of you," added Davis.

"Lieutenant," said Gatewood, a warning in his tone of voice. It was enough. Davis felt himself to be properly chastised.

"Don't you sass me, bluecoat," said Hawkins. He waited a moment, and when Davis did not respond, he assumed that he had cowed the young officer. He turned his head to look again at Geronimo, and then he took a couple of steps toward the warrior.

"The great Geronimo," he said with a sneer. "Well, I don't think you're nothing but a murdering red bastard."

Geronimo was on his feet in an instant, his cocked Colt .45 revolver held out at arm's length pointed directly at Hawkins's chest. Hawkins froze in his tracks, his face registering astonished horror. The deputy's eyes popped open wide with fear.

Mangas and Ulzana, following the lead of Geronimo, stood, lifted their Winchesters, and levered cartridges into the chambers. They covered the two lawmen, holding the rifles ready to fire. There was a moment of intense silence. Gatewood walked over close to Hawkins, standing between the lawmen and the Apaches.

"You going to let him get away with this?" said Hawkins, his voice trembling with rage and fear. "You just going to let them level down like that on a white man?"

"On two white men," corrected the deputy.

"I'd ride on out of here if I were you, sir," said Gatewood, his voice calm. "You seem to have provoked . . . the hostiles, and I certainly don't think you want any problems with the United States Army. Do you?"

Hawkins backed away toward the door, keeping his eyes on Geronimo, bumping into his deputy. He turned partially around and shoved the little man toward the door. "Let me tell you something, soldier," he said. "Even the U.S. Army is subject to a federal warrant. You know that? Justice is going to be served—one way or the other. You ain't heard the last of this. No, sir. You ain't heard the last."

He turned quickly and pushed his weasely deputy out through the door, hurrying out himself, nearly running over the smaller man. Still standing quietly at the window, Chato watched the two hurriedly and clumsily mount up and ride away fast into the setting sun. Gatewood stepped over to stand beside Chato, his field glasses in his hand. He raised the glasses to watch the retreating lawmen.

Geronimo eased the hammer forward on his Colt and dropped it back into the holster. His companions, following his lead, lowered their rifles. Geronimo smiled at Gatewood's back. This one will be all right, he thought. He's a good soldier. At the same time, Geronimo almost regretted that Gatewood had prevented him from killing the two ugly white men. They had asked for it. They deserved killing, and Geronimo would have enjoyed obliging them.

"We move," Gatewood said. "Tonight. If we can get a big enough lead, maybe they won't catch up with us."

Chapter 4

It was gray dawn, and the nine riders had been traveling hard all night with no sleep and precious little rest. Davis thought that the great expanse of nothingness seemed as if it had no end. The night had been cold, and the morning was still cool, but Davis had by this time been in the desert long enough to know that the day would soon grow hot, almost unbearably so before it was over. Still, he was glad for the light. The nighttime travel in the unfamiliar desert had been eerie and more than a little frightening.

Chato rode up beside Gatewood and pointed to their rear. Gatewood called a halt to the little column and took out his field glasses. He looked through them and found what Chato had indicated.

"It's that damned Hawkins all right," said the

lieutenant, "and he's got his posse. I count fifteen of them, and that looks like Yaqui Dave leading them. He's a tracker, and a damn good one, I'm sorry to say. He used to work for the army. I'm afraid they've caught our trail, Mr. Davis."

"Yes, sir?" Looking forward to his military career, Davis had not ever anticipated being pursued in his own country by a legal posse possessed of a valid United States warrant. He wondered what Gatewood would do if it came to a showdown with these lawmen. Then, recalling the way the sleazy bastards had behaved back at the stage depot, he thought, if the lieutenant tells me to shoot them, by God, I will.

Gatewood put away his glasses. "We'll move to the higher ground," he said, pointing. "Over there near the rocks. We'll be harder to track there."

Geronimo took out his own battered field glasses, stolen from a dead soldier, to have a look for himself. He saw Yaqui Dave, small and wiry, dressed in greasy buckskins, riding twenty yards ahead of the posse. He knew this Yaqui Dave, a good tracker. They would not be able to hide their trail from him, not with the two White-eye soldiers along. They would have to do something else, he knew. He put away his glasses and turned to ride along with the others.

Chato led the way toward the plateaus that rose above the desert floor ahead of them. As they were about to go up the steep rise, Gatewood dropped out of line and waved them on. Geronimo also dropped out and moved over to Gatewood's side.

As the rest of the column moved toward the top of the mesa, Gatewood again took out his glasses to scan the horizon behind them. He had lost sight of their pursuers.

"You see them?" Gatewood asked.

Geronimo was looking through his own glasses. Holding them with one hand, he pointed with the other.

"There," Geronimo said.

Gatewood looked where Geronimo indicated, then moved his glasses and found Yaqui Dave in them. The tracker was on the ground examining the trail, and the rest of the posse was moving up close behind him.

"What do you see there, Dave boy?" asked the weasel-faced deputy.

"Eight or nine of them," said Dave.

"I thought Apaches was supposed to hide their damn tracks," said Hawkins.

"Not if they're on the run," said the tracker. "Besides, these have got two white men with them. Soldiers."

"Yeah," said Hawkins. "I know about them two soldiers."

The deputy bared his teeth in a wide grin.

"Did you hear what he said, Joe? We got them on the run," he said in his high-pitched nasal voice. He reached into his saddlebag and brought out a whiskey jug, uncorked it, and took a long pull. Then he wiped his mouth on his sleeve.

"Ah," he said, "that's damn good stuff."

"Give me a swig," said Hawkins, and the deputy handed him the jug.

Gatewood and Geronimo had ridden on up to the top of the mesa to join the others, and there again, Gatewood searched for the posse with his glasses. This time Davis stood beside him. Gatewood lowered the glasses, but continued to stare in the direction of the posse.

"They've still got hold of our trail," he said. "We can't shake that Yaqui Dave. No way. We're going to have to think of something else."

"Can we outrun them?" asked Davis.

"Not with the pack mules," said Gatewood.

"We could abandon the mules."

"An army officer does not abandon his supply train without a fight, Mr. Davis," said Gatewood. He stared out across the alkali flat below toward the pursuing posse. He knew that he had to make some kind of decision, and he had to make it soon.

They had not lost the posse, apparently could not, and the lieutenant knew that they could not outrun them. He also knew that Hawkins would kill Geronimo, and perhaps the rest of them, if he caught up with them. If he were to lose Geronimo, Gatewood thought, especially to that bunch, he would probably be better off letting Hawkins kill him than facing General Crook with the embarrassing news. At the very least, he would have to look for a new career. He made his decision.

"Mr. Davis," Gatewood said, "as a decoying maneuver, you will continue north with Geronimo and the others. If I don't rejoin you by sundown, you will escort the group on to San Carlos. Chato will go with you to show you the way."

"Sir?" said Davis. "Not to question your orders, but—"

"Then Mr. Davis," Gatewood snapped, "do not question my orders. I'm making a rear-guard protective stand right here." He turned toward Geronimo who was standing nearby. "I want you and your men to go with Mr. Davis," he continued. "I'm staying here. I have to figure out some way to deal with this posse."

"I'll stay with you," said Geronimo.

"My orders are to see that you get delivered to Nantan Lupan," said Gatewood, his exasperation clear in his voice.

"I stay here," said Geronimo, and his voice was calm but firm. "With you."

Gatewood gave Geronimo a hard look, but the Apache warrior returned his stare. Gatewood knew he couldn't win this contest. He gave it up. At least if Geronimo fell into the hands of the posse, Gatewood would die there with him. He wouldn't have to face General Crook or look for a new career. He wondered what the military history books would say about this one.

The plateau turned into a rock shelf leading to the face of cliffs which rose even higher above. Gatewood and Geronimo had climbed to the top of the cliffs. They watched for a while as the mule train and the other men led by Chato rode hard across the plateau. He thought about the irony of his situation, defending a position against lawmen, in the company of Geronimo.

Then Gatewood lifted his glasses and turned his attention back to the posse still in the open country even farther below. He watched them for a moment, then put his glasses down and turned toward Geronimo.

"If they serve those warrants," he said, "I'll have to give you up. I'll have no choice. A federal warrant is like an order. But that's more of a lynch mob down there than a posse. If they get their hands on you, I don't think they'll take you back to Tombstone alive to stand trial."

Geronimo looked at Gatewood's field glasses, and held his own over beside them for comparison.

"You have a very good long glass, Gatewood," he said.

Gatewood wondered if Geronimo had any idea of the import of what he had been telling him. He certainly didn't show any interest in the words.

Geronimo put the glasses down and picked up his Sharps rifle. His Winchester was also lying close by. He set up the tang sight on his Sharps, and again he looked through his glasses at the posse. He remembered Hawkins from the depot, recalled how the man had spoken to him, how he had looked at him with hate burning in his bloodshot eyes.

"I'll scare them off," Geronimo said, "if you trade me the long glass."

Gatewood stared at him for a moment. There were fifteen mounted, heavily armed men down below who wanted nothing more than to kill this man, and he was calmly bargaining for a pair of field glasses. "I can't let you kill any of these men," he said.

While Geronimo lifted his glasses for another look, Yaqui Dave rode to the base of the plateau down below and motioned for the posse to hold up. He swung down off his horse and looked at the ground. He walked ahead, checking the signs. It was a good trail. He pointed up toward the top of the mesa.

"What do you see, Dave?" said Hawkins.

Geronimo cocked his Sharps, felt the breeze, and adjusted the sight. He waited. He wanted to make the first shot count. He wanted just the right shot.

Yaqui Dave and the posse reached the top of the mesa. They were about 150 yards from the face of the cliff. He motioned them forward. Hawkins hurried to catch up with him.

"What do you think?" Hawkins asked, red-faced and puffing for breath.

Yaqui Dave pointed toward the cliffs. "Up there," he said. "Looks like they split off. Six or seven of them headed on toward San Carlos. The other two's up yonder."

Hawkins reached a hand out toward his toothy deputy, who had ridden up beside him by then, and, keeping his eyes on the cliffs ahead, said, "Pass me that God-damned jug."

The deputy dug out the whiskey jug and handed it over to Hawkins, who uncorked it and raised it to his lips to drink. Suddenly the jug exploded sending a shower of shards and a spray of whiskey over Hawkins's face and shirt front. Then he heard the boom of the distant shot.

Up on the cliff, Geronimo smiled. He started to reload the Sharps.

"That was a great shot," said Gatewood.

"Not so great," said Geronimo. "I aimed for his head."

He put aside the Sharps and picked up his Winchester. Gatewood lifted his own Winchester, and the two began to fire at the posse as fast as they could lever cartridges into their chambers. Gatewood was not aiming at anyone. His intention was only to scatter the posse and frighten them into a disorderly retreat. He hoped that Geronimo shared with him those same intentions. The bastards probably deserved killing, but Gatewood couldn't let that happen. Not on this occasion. It was not always easy or pleasant upholding the official position on matters.

The mounted posse members screamed and shouted and raced around in all directions, but when Yaqui Dave hurried his mount down into the protection of a small arroyo, the others, even in their fright and confusion, managed to find their way in after him. The shots from above slowed some then, and Hawkins, panting for breath, stared hard toward the cliff. Yaqui Dave turned in the saddle to face Hawkins.

"My guess is that's Geronimo up there," he said. "Well, I found them for you. I earned my money.

Now you don't need me to serve your damn warrants."

Ducking low over his horse's neck, Yaqui Dave rode out of the arroyo as fast as he could and then headed away from the cliffs. A few shots kicked up dust near him as he rode, but they only served to make him ride faster.

From the relative safety of the arroyo, Hawkins and his deputy continued to stare at the cliffs above. The others still milled around, all seeming to talk at once. The arroyo was filled with a mass of confusion.

"What do you think, Joe?" asked the deputy, his eyes wide and his quivering voice full of fear.

Two more shots rang out, and the lawmen ducked their heads as dirt flew in their faces.

"God damn," whined the weasel-faced deputy.

"Hell, I don't know," said Hawkins. "Ain't no damn way we can rush them. We'd just go and get ourselves killed. That's all."

There was another boom, and then another, followed by a long, rolling echo across the dunes.

"Let's go chase that other bunch," said the deputy.

"Hell," said Hawkins, "they got a damn good head start on us by now, and besides, there's more of them than there are of these here."

There was another rifle shot, and somewhere in the crowded arroyo a posse member screamed in pain. A horse reared, spooked, and all of a sudden confusion and chaos ruled in the ranks of the posse. Men tried to turn their horses. Horses ran into each other. A man fell off the back of his horse and huddled into a ball on the ground for fear of being trampled to death. Men shouted and cursed, and horses neighed their fear and confusion.

"Who's hit?" yelled Hawkins.

"Me," answered a voice from the mob. "My shoulder's broke, and I'm bleeding to death."

"Let's get the damn hell out of here," shouted Hawkins. "God-damn army."

He turned his horse to race out of the arroyo, and he was followed close behind by the toothy deputy and the rest of the posse. Bullets whined and kicked up dust on both sides of them, as they rode hard on the already retreating trail of Yaqui Dave.

Up above, Gatewood and Geronimo watched the departing horsemen grow smaller as they hurried toward the far horizon. Gatewood stood up.

"We'd best catch up with Mr. Davis and the others," he said.

"You don't have to worry about Davis," said Geronimo. "My men will protect him."

Gatewood paused and looked at Geronimo, held up his field glasses, and studied them for a moment, then held them out toward Geronimo. "Trade," he said.

Geronimo took the glasses and handed his own to Gatewood. He then lifted his new glasses and looked at the embossed name on the leather case. "This is your name, Gatewood?" he asked.

"Yes," said Gatewood. "The glasses were a gift from my troops."

Geronimo lifted the new glasses to his eyes and studied the retreating horsemen still visible on the horizon. He lowered them again, and he smiled. Gatewood felt some mild irritation toward the Apache. He couldn't be sure if Geronimo's smile was more a result of the quality of the glasses or of the fact that he had managed to get them from Gatewood by means of a slick trade.

"They must think you're a fine chief, Gatewood," said Geronimo.

"Not a chief," said Gatewood. "Only a soldier."

"Your long glass is better than mine," said Geronimo, and he pulled a small buckskin pouch out from inside his waistband. He opened the pouch and poured several brilliant blue chunks of azurite into his hand. He selected the largest one and held it out toward Gatewood. "The blue stone is valuable to the Apaches," he said.

Gatewood took the stone. "Thank you," he said.

Geronimo lifted his new glasses to his eyes and looked out across the landscape.

Chapter 5

The San Carlos Agency was located at the convergence of the Gila and San Carlos rivers where a dry and gravelly mesa rose thirty or more feet above the river bottoms. The agency buildings, all of adobe, were located on top of the mesa. There were scattered cottonwood trees along the edges of streams, but there was almost no other vegetation. Hot, dry winds constantly sloughed across the barren flats.

A trooper standing on lookout atop the mesa stiffened and squinted his eyes against the brightness of the sun. He had seen movement in the distance. He waited until he could see it more clearly as it came closer. Then he shouted.

"Detail coming."

Another soldier ran over to his side. "How many?" he asked anxiously.

"Nine in all," said the sentry. "Two in uniform."

As the second soldier ran toward the headquarters building to report, others, soldiers not on duty and civilians, came out to look. There was not much excitement at San Carlos. Someone's arrival —anyone's—was big news at the desolate post.

Down on the flat, Gatewood led his small column at an easy pace toward the mesa. He slowed his own mount just a bit in order to allow Davis to come up alongside him, and then he pointed to the mesa looming before them in the distance.

"There it is, Mr. Davis," he said. "Your new home."

"San Carlos?" said Davis.

"That's right."

Then they heard the faint sounds of a bugle cutting through the oppressive desert air.

"That sounds like they're preparing our welcoming committee," Gatewood said.

"I hope there's a bathtub available," said Davis. "That's the best welcome I can think of."

He was tired and worn down from the long ride, days in the saddle, the severe contrast of cold nights and burning hot days and the desert dust caked on his skin. And he could not help but notice that the Apaches did not seem to be tired at all. They rode comfortably, as if they had just left their homes that morning for a short ride into town. He was glad that he had arrived in time for Geronimo's surrender, for he could see that these Apaches would have made formidable enemies indeed.

When Gatewood at last led his detachment into the agency compound, three companies of cavalry waited at spit-and-polish attention, and an eight-piece military band began to play. Davis was struck by the drabness of the post. The surroundings were just like the rest of the desert, except, of course, for the squat adobe structures, and there was water. He asked himself what he had been expecting, and the only answer he could come up with was perhaps some relief from the harsh environment. He guessed he had found it, such as it was.

Of course, he figured, soon he would be able to take the bath he longed for, and he would be able to get some much-needed rest in a real bed, even if it was only an army cot. When he dressed again, it would be in a clean, fresh uniform. He decided that was all the relief he would need.

At the same time, as he was considering the misery of his personal condition and of his surroundings, Davis could not help himself from feeling a strong sense of patriotic pride swelling his breast from deep within. The troops were all standing at attention to greet him, the band was playing; all stirred his blood. No one at San Carlos knew him, but he was riding in to report to his new post in the company of the famous Geronimo.

As he looked around, Davis noticed a small crowd on the porch of one of the buildings to the side. The group seemed to be made up of officers' wives and children, and possibly a few civilians. He imagined that everyone at the post had turned out for this occasion.

Then Gatewood called a halt in front of another building, and Davis saw a man come out the door to stand under the overhanging porch roof. He was dressed in the white canvas uniform of the sort usually worn by cavalrymen on stable detail, and he was straightening a white cork sun helmet on his head. He sported a magnificent forked beard, which at one time had been a dark brown but was liberally streaked with gray. His clothes hung loosely on him, giving him a casual, even sloppy, appearance.

Gatewood saluted. "General," he said.

So this, thought Davis, is the famous General George Crook. Davis had, of course, heard of Crook's many eccentricities, but even so, he had not been prepared for the sight of the humble uniform and the decidedly unmilitary manner. Crook was a major celebrity with a sterling reputation as an Indian fighter, and it was widely known that he had been rated by General William Tecumseh Sherman as his best field commander.

Davis suddenly felt as if he were living a West Point cadet's dream with General Crook in front of him and Geronimo behind him, two of the most famous men of the West. This would be a day to remember, one to tell his grandchildren about some day. Certainly, it was something to write to his mother about. The general's voice intruded into Davis's thoughts.

"My compliments, Lieutenant," said Crook to Gatewood.

Then Davis heard some gasps from the onlookers and saw their eyes staring at something behind him. He turned to look and saw that Geronimo had pulled the Sharps rifle from its scabbard and had moved out of line to ride forward. He rode on up to stop beside Gatewood, and he threw a leg over his white horse and dropped to the ground to stand in front of Crook. He held the Sharps out toward Crook.

"Nantan Lupan," Geronimo said, and he looked the general in the eyes. Davis thought that Geronimo did not have the look or manner of a man who was surrendering. His bearing was proud and noble. He seemed more like a visiting dignitary from some exotic land.

Crook reached out and took the weapon from Geronimo's hands. "It does my heart good to see you, Geronimo," he said, and he seemed genuinely friendly and pleased. "I accept your surrender," he continued. "I accept the surrender of a great warrior."

The General stepped aside, gesturing toward the front door of the headquarters building with his right hand, still holding Geronimo's Sharps rifle in his left. "Let's have some coffee," he said. "Smoke cigars. We have a lot to talk about."

Geronimo walked beside Crook toward the door. Gatewood and Davis followed close behind. Al Sieber was lounging on the porch leaning casually against a post. Geronimo saw him, stopped in front of him, and looked him in the eyes.

"Well," said Sieber, "it's old Geronimo. Good to see you. Ain't it?"

Sieber moved the chaw of tobacco from one cheek to the other and smiled.

"I think you know Al Sieber," said Crook.

Geronimo continued to stare into Sieber's eyes. He said nothing. He knew Sieber, all right. He knew him well. He knew him not only as a man who killed Apaches, but also as a man who enlisted Apaches to kill other Apaches. He knew him, all right, and he hated him.

"I was always hoping to catch up with you myself," said the chief of scouts. "Guess I'll never get the chance now, or will I?"

"Come along," said Crook, and he led Geronimo to the door and opened it, standing to one side. Geronimo walked in. Sieber watched until his old enemy disappeared from view. Then he spat a brown stream into the dust in front of the porch.

Inside the office, a soldier stood up to attention behind a desk. Crook spoke to him from out on the porch through the open door.

"See that Geronimo gets a good cup of coffee," said Crook.

"Yes, sir."

Gatewood and Davis had come in behind Crook, and as the general turned away from the open doorway, they found themselves facing him, standing close.

"My compliments, sir," said Gatewood. "It's a good day all around."

"You aren't entirely convinced though that this will work, are you, Lieutenant?" said Crook.

"I think this is the best chance the Apaches have,

sir," Gatewood answered diplomatically. "As to whether or not it will work—well, nobody knows."

"Um, yes," said Crook. He turned to go inside.

"Sir?"

"Yes?"

The general paused in the doorway and turned back to face Gatewood.

"May I present Lieutenant Davis?"

"Oh, yes, of course," said Crook.

Davis snapped to attention and saluted, and Crook returned the salute in his usual casual manner.

"Second Lieutenant Britton Davis, sir," said Davis.

"Welcome to San Carlos, Mr. Davis," said the general. "Now both of you come on inside."

Davis was given a cup of coffee and left in the outer office. Gatewood accompanied Crook into a large squad room, which contained several desks and filing cabinets and a number of straight-backed chairs. A sentry stood at the door, and Geronimo was sitting in the room alone. A cup of coffee was on the table beside him.

"Shut the door, Lieutenant," said Crook. Gatewood shut the door, leaving the sentry on the other side. Then he took a place against the wall just beside the door. Crook walked over to face Geronimo, who remained seated. A friendly smile spread across Crook's face. He seemed to be greeting an old friend.

"I'm glad to see that Geronimo is a man of his word," said Crook. He took several cigars out of a box on a desk top and handed them to Geronimo, who looked them over, took one out, and put the others into a shirt pocket. "Washington has ordered me to detain you here at San Carlos for a short period and then to send you and your band of Chiricahuas on over to Turkey Creek."

Geronimo looked at Crook skeptically. This was what he had asked for. It was what he had been promised. He had a tendency to believe this man, Nantan Lupan, but he had been lied to before by the White-eyes. He was not quite sure that this one was really any different, even though he was a good soldier. Crook struck a match on the table top and held the flame out in his cupped hands. Geronimo put the cigar in his mouth and leaned slightly forward to accept the light. He took several puffs to make sure he had it going well.

"It's a good smoke," he said. "We keep our rifles for hunting?"

"Yes," said Crook. "But hunting on the reservation only. I'll put one of my officers in charge there—"

"Gatewood," said Geronimo.

Gatewood, still standing back out of the way, heard the request with a surprise bordering on disbelief, and his mind recalled the incident with the posse out in the desert. Still, he had told Geronimo to his face that he wanted to kill him.

"No," said Crook. "I'm sorry, but I need Lieutenant Gatewood close by. He's my right hand."

"Then we'll take Davis," said Geronimo. He puffed on his cigar, and clouds of rich smoke hung about his head. "I like Davis."

"I'm sure that Mr. Davis is going to make a fine officer one of these days," said Crook, "but I had somebody more experienced in mind."

"I like Davis," said Geronimo. He picked up the cup and sipped some coffee from it. He set it back down and puffed on the cigar. The room was beginning to fill with smoke.

Crook crossed his arms and paced away, then back again. He looked past Geronimo to Gatewood, still standing back against the wall.

"What do you think, Lieutenant?" he asked.

Gatewood stepped forward to stand beside Geronimo, facing Crook.

"I'm sure it will be his privilege as well as his duty," he said.

Crook smiled and nodded.

"Then Mr. Davis it is," he said, "with a small detachment of soldiers. The Apaches at Turkey Creek will continue to be under the protection of the United States Army."

Geronimo drank down the rest of the coffee and put the cup back on the table. He stood up, poked the cigar back in his mouth and, puffing, looked Crook in the face.

"Mr. Davis is young," said Crook. "Young Apaches. Young White-eyes. They're the hope of the West."

"Davis," said Geronimo. He smiled and gave a nod. "He's okay."

"I hope the wars are over, my friend," Crook continued. "I hope the Apaches and the White-eyes can live in peace from here on. Nantan Lupan wants the Apaches to learn to be farmers. It's their only chance. They must change. The old days are gone."

While Crook was talking, Geronimo had decided that the meeting was over. He didn't want to hear the general talk about the need for Apaches to learn to be farmers. They had always been farmers, but Geronimo knew what Nantan Lupan meant. He meant that he wanted them to learn to be farmers the way that white men were farmers. He pretended not to be listening, and he turned as if to leave the room, but he paused for a moment, facing Gatewood.

"Gatewood," he said, "will you come and visit me at Turkey Creek?"

Gatewood studied the hard, dark face there in front of him for a moment, the face of a man he had said he wanted to kill, the face of a man who had killed his friends. But it was also now the face of a man who had fought by his side.

"Yes," he said. "I would like that."

And the lieutenant was surprised to find that he actually meant what he had said. Had he also been looking into the face of . . . a friend?

Chapter 6

Looking out across a wide plateau to a distant horizon, Turkey Creek was a more pleasant environment than any Davis had experienced since his arrival in Arizona Territory. Not far from the mountains, with a fresh stream running through, its temperature was more mild than that at San Carlos. There was more and greener vegetation. He had seen immediately upon his arrival why Geronimo had insisted upon this spot for his reservation.

Davis and the other soldiers had set up tents, and the Apaches had constructed wickieups, each a framework of poles and limbs tied together and covered over by a thatch of bear grass, yucca leaves, and brush, the top left open for a smoke hole. The army had supplied the Apaches with canvas, and this was stretched over the entire structure. Davis's tent, larger than those of the other soldiers, was also set apart from them and was surrounded by about fifty wickieups.

Davis was a little surprised to find himself so comfortable with his new assignment. He couldn't have been more pleased with the way his career was getting started. Before ever even reaching his post, he had joined a small detachment sent out to escort Geronimo back to San Carlos. Then he had actually received the special assignment of commanding the troops in charge of Geronimo and his band at Turkey Creek.

He had a small command, and he was getting along well with both his soldiers and the Apaches. He found that he didn't at all mind living in the tent. It was roomy and contained a cot and a table and chairs.

As soon as the camp had been established and everyone had a place to live, Davis called a meeting of all the Apaches. They gathered at the edge of the encampment. Geronimo and old Nana sat in front. Davis stood up before them all to speak. His small detachment of troopers and Apache scouts stood off to one side. Sergeant Turkey stood beside Davis to serve as his translator.

"**Nantan Lupan says,**" Davis began, "there must be no leaving the reservation for even a few hours without permission. There must be no drinking of whiskey or *tizwin*. Any violation of these rules will be punishable by confinement in an army prison stockade."

Davis paused to allow Sergeant Turkey to translate, and as the scout finished speaking, old Nana stood up and spoke.

"What is this?" he said, speaking in Apache. "Why worry if Apaches get drunk too?"

Davis looked at Sergeant Turkey.

"He wants to know why these rules," said the scout. "Why are we being punished? What you care if Apaches drink? Soldiers drink. Why do you treat us like children?"

"Nantan Lupan says if Apaches drink," said Davis, "Apaches fight. Apaches get in trouble. It's bad for everyone. Bad for Apaches. Bad for soldiers. Bad for all White-eyes."

Sergeant Turkey translated and again old Nana spoke out.

"Why do all of us have to pay if a few Apaches cause trouble?" he asked in Apache.

"He wants to know why," said Sergeant Turkey, "if some Apaches do bad things, all are punished."

"That will not happen," said Davis. "All Apaches should not be punished for the mistakes of a few. If we can determine those responsible, only they will be punished. Nantan Lupan is fair. He keeps his word."

Davis had been at Turkey Creek for about six weeks when Gatewood and Sieber, accompanied by a squad of soldiers and a few Apache scouts, came riding into his camp. Sieber spotted Mangas across the way and turned to ride directly over to him. He didn't bother stopping to acknowledge Davis. Mangas saw him coming. He had been watching the movements of all the White-eyes since they had ridden into the camp. Sieber pulled up a few feet away from where Mangas sat.

"Hello, Mangas," he said. "You're just the fellow I want to see."

Mangas looked warily at his old enemy. He did not like this white man; he did not trust him either. This man had killed many Apaches. Mangas would much have preferred fighting him than having a conversation with him. He sat quietly, though, keeping his thoughts to himself, his face betraying nothing of his feelings.

"I want you to come with me and join the army," said Sieber. "Be a wolf with a blue coat. Scout for us and help us fight renegades." He paused and smiled. "I'll make you a sergeant," he continued. "You'll wear a blue coat with stripes on your sleeve, and you'll get army pay. Well, what do you say?"

"I don't know, Sieber," said Mangas.

"Hell," said Sieber, "you're a warrior, Mangas, a manhunter. Wear a blue coat, and make your woman proud. Make your children proud of their daddy."

"Mexicans took my wife," said Mangas, "and my little boy."

"Well, there you go," said Sieber. "Maybe the army can help you get them back."

Mangas looked up at Sieber and felt a moment of weakness. A glimmer of hope was in his eyes, and Sieber saw indecision in the Apache warrior's face. By God, I've got him, he thought.

"The army would do this?" Mangas asked.

"They could try. It all depends on how much you cooperate, now, don't it?"

Mangas sat silent for a while. This Sieber is like a snake, he thought. He did not think that he would like cooperating with Sieber.

"I think maybe I'll just stay here," he said.

Sieber's jaws tightened in anger, and he jerked the reins of his mount to turn it and ride away.

"I guess you just ain't quite ready," he said. "Hell, if I was asking you to go out on a damned raiding party, I expect you'd be a lot more willing."

He rode off, his horse's hoofs kicking dust and clods of earth back toward where Mangas sat.

"No. Not with you, I wouldn't," Mangas said quietly. "Not with you, Sieber."

Gatewood rode slowly through the cluster of wickieups and ramadas on his way to find Geronimo. Children ran alongside his horse laughing and playing. A woman tossed out a bowl of dirty water in front of him, and an old man waved a greeting. Dogs barked. Most of the people, though, sat with sullen faces, watching as he rode by. It was the kind of reception he expected.

Then he saw Geronimo seated in front of a wickieup, and he rode on over there and dismounted. A smile played across Geronimo's face.

"Gatewood," he said. "You come to visit me."

"It does my heart good to see Geronimo," said Gatewood.

Geronimo stood up, and Gatewood reached into a pocket for a handful of cigars. He held them out toward Geronimo, who took them, selected one, and pocketed the others.

"How's the life of a farmer?" Gatewood asked.

Geronimo bit off the end of his cigar and spat it out.

"Some Apaches are good farmers," he said. "Others—they miss the old ways."

Gatewood knew that Geronimo was talking about himself. He struck a match on the sole of his boot and held it out toward Geronimo in cupped hands. Geronimo leaned forward and lit his cigar. He took a few puffs to get it going good, then leaned back and exhaled a big cloud with obvious pleasure.

"I'm not a very good farmer, Gatewood," he said.

"Some of my family were farmers," said the lieutenant. "Some were soldiers. The farmers were much happier. They ate better." He held up the blue stone that Geronimo had given him that day on the mesa in the desert. "I think I should send the blue stone to my wife," he said.

"You have babies?" Geronimo asked. "The blue stone will make them strong."

"Two children," said Gatewood. "They are with my wife, a long way from here. More than a thousand miles."

"You should be with your family," said Geronimo. "A wife and babies need to be near the father."

Geronimo thought about his own babies, killed long ago in Mexico, along with the young wife he had so cherished. He could not even remember well what they had looked like in life. He had only a grim image of the bodies he had discovered, an image which still haunted him and still fed the hatred he carried in his heart against the Mexicans.

"Now that the war's over," said Gatewood, "maybe I'll have that chance."

Geronimo puffed on the cigar. Then he made a half turn and a sweeping motion with his arm toward the mountains beyond.

"I was born near here," he said, "beyond those mountains. My mother rolled me on the ground in the four directions. It's our way, so the child will be connected to the land."

Gatewood paused for a moment before speaking. He knew something of what was in Geronimo's mind. It was something to do with the Apaches' love of their land, and the white man's coming to steal it away from them. He knew what his uniform represented to Geronimo and to all the Apaches. He looked at the mountains, then back down at the ground where he stood, the ground that he was helping the United States government secure by conquering the Apaches.

"I came here to visit my friend," he said, "but there are questions I have to ask." Gatewood felt guilty at his small lie. He would not have made the trip just to visit Geronimo. He wondered if Geronimo could read the lie. "There are rumors going around," the lieutenant continued, "about an Apache medicine man speaking against the White-eyes. They say that he's calling for a return to the war trail."

"It was told by an Apache medicine man," said Geronimo, "that many more Apaches will die fighting the White-eyes. And in the end, we will win, because we will die free of them."

"The only way an Apache can be free is to die?" asked Gatewood. He heaved a sigh. "Which medicine man? I should talk to him. I should find out what he's saying."

"There are many of them," said Geronimo. "Some have the power. Some just talk."

Gatewood had a powerful feeling that Geronimo knew exactly which medicine man the army was interested in, but he wasn't about to divulge any information. He knew, too, that any attempt on his part to try to pry more out of the tough old veteran would be useless. He was afraid the war would start again.

"I wonder," Gatewood said, "if the medicine man had any babies."

Looking out toward the mountains, Geronimo puffed on his cigar.

Gatewood and the others who had come with him were still at the Turkey Creek camp at sundown. Gatewood was inside Davis's tent. The two officers sat at the table eating. For light, a lantern burned on the table.

"You and Geronimo seem to get along pretty well," said Davis.

"I think he trusts me," said Gatewood.

"Begging your pardon, sir," said Davis, "but why would he? I mean, you know, the uniform and all."

Gatewood finished chewing a mouthful and swallowed. He washed it down with a sip of coffee.

It was a damned good question. He had asked it of himself more than once.

"I don't know," he said. "Maybe because I know what it's like for the United States Cavalry to burn your home. Maybe it's because I know what it's like to want to fight the bluecoats to the death. Maybe it's something else entirely. I don't know."

Davis gave Gatewood a puzzled look.

"Sir?" Davis said. "Did you say, you know what it's like to want to fight the bluecoats—to the death?"

Gatewood's face took on a sudden faraway look, and when he spoke again, he didn't really seem to be speaking to Davis, but there was no one else around to hear.

"My two older brothers and my father fought for the Army of Northern Virginia," he said. "One brother was killed. My father was wounded, crippled for life."

After a moment of uneasy silence, Davis asked, "Why did you . . . come over to our side, sir?"

"I'm a soldier," said Gatewood, his voice back to normal. "It's the only side left."

They heard the crunch of approaching footsteps outside, and in another moment Al Sieber came into the tent unasked and unannounced. He grabbed a campaign chair and straddled it, leaning his arms on the top of the chair back.

"You got a drink in here, Davis?" he asked.

"There's no whiskey on this reservation," said Davis. "It's against army regulations. You know that."

"I finished up my private stash last night," said Sieber. "You don't keep something on the side?"

"Maybe you didn't hear me," said Davis. "There's no whiskey on this reservation."

"None for them," said Sieber, gesturing out toward the Apache wickieups. "Hell, I know that. But you know—a little something on the side for a traveling White-eye . . ."

He looked at Davis and instantly read the disapproval in the young officer's face.

"Christ," he said. "I guess the God-damned army just ain't what it used to be." He heaved a heavy sigh and turned to Gatewood. "How's your friend Geronimo?" he asked.

"He doesn't like being a farmer," said Gatewood.

"What's he say about the medicine man?"

"He says some have the power, some just talk."

"I tell you," said Sieber, "something's going on. I can tell you that. I can smell it."

At the far end of the camp, a small fire burned in front of the wickieup of Geronimo. Around the fire sat Geronimo, old Nana, Mangas, and Ulzana. The sky was dark, and they could see the figures of the two officers and the scout silhouetted inside Davis's tent. They spoke in low voices in their native tongue.

"Long ago," said old Nana, "before the white people came, it was good. We lived in a good way. We had many friends. There was food everywhere, and we didn't have to be afraid to go get it. But now we have to stay here, while the white people cut down trees and dig in the earth and shoot everything that lives—every wild animal."

"Even here," said Ulzana, "we must do as they say, but white people do what they want to do. Bad people walk around, but good people cannot. You can't hunt. You can't make *tutbai*. You can't complain. If you do, they arrest you. They take you away. Some people never come back."

"The medicine man at Cibecue," said Mangas, "is called the Dreamer. He says all the White-eyes are evil. He says the dead chiefs will rise."

Geronimo puffed on his cigar. He had heard all of this before. He had said it himself, many times.

"Last night," he said, "I looked into my power. I saw a trail of dead Apaches, and bluecoats were standing in their blood. Nantan Lupan was standing in their blood."

Chapter 7

Back at San Carlos, General George Crook, also known as Nantan Lupan or the Gray Wolf by the Apaches, sat on the porch of his headquarters building behind a campaign desk covered with papers, watching the cavalry troops at drill on the parade ground. It was a bright day, with the sun strong overhead. The heat was oppressive, and a wide variety of insects swarmed around the general's head. Around the cluster of adobe buildings, chickens wandered free, pecking and clucking. Dogs slept in the shade, or tried to, and children ran and played. People of all kinds, white civilians, soldiers' wives and children, Indians, and Mexicans lounged around watching the spectacle on the parade ground.

Captain Hentig, Sergeant Mulrey, an aide-de-camp named Howard, and a civilian white man approached the porch at a fast walking pace, the civilian puffing to keep step with the military stride. Crook waited until they had stopped in front of him below the porch. Then he looked up from his papers.

"Captain Hentig," he said.

"Sir," said Hentig, stepping out of line and up onto the porch.

"Take Al Sieber with you," said Crook, "and go on up to Cibecue. I have some more reports here about a medicine man causing trouble up there. See what you can find out."

"Yes, sir," said Hentig.

"Find him if you can, and take him into custody if you have to," said Crook. "I don't want any damn medicine man giving ideas to the Apaches about taking up the war path again. That's the last damn thing in the world I want. Do you understand, Captain?"

"Yes, sir," said Hentig, delivering a snappy salute. Crook lazily returned the salute and looked over to where some Apache scouts were lounging in the sparse shade of a nearby squat adobe.

"Dead Shot," he shouted.

A scout wearing a battered white top hat trotted easily over to the porch, and came to a halt in front of Crook.

"Nantan Lupan," he said.

"You're from Cibecue," said Crook. "You lead the scouts. How long have you worked for me, Dead Shot?"

"Seven years," said Dead Shot.

"And you love that hat almost as much as you love me," said Crook. The statement was delivered in a totally serious tone of voice, and the general's face was stern.

"I love my wife and baby," said the scout. "Then I love Nantan Lupan. Then I love my hat."

"That's a good answer," said Crook. He dismissed Dead Shot and the rest of Hentig's command with a wave of his hand. "Mr. Howard," he said.

Aide-de-camp Howard, still standing off the porch, stepped forward.

"Sir," he said, "by your order, Mr. Howles, the government agent is here."

Crook looked up at Howles for the first time. The man was overweight and soft-looking. His red, puffy face showed that he suspected that something was up, and he did not appear to be happy about it. Crook could tell that the man was on the defensive before anything had even been said. He did not like the man and certainly did not want to waste time in conversation with him. He decided to get right to the point.

"Howles," he said abruptly, "you're fired. I've checked into your records. Audited your books. You're just another thief. And not even a clever one. Back in the time of Cochise, if somebody cheated the Apaches in a business deal, Cochise'd have his eyes beaten out with stones. Think about it, Mr. Howles. Why would a blind man need so much money?"

"Now wait a minute. You just hold on a minute

there, General," protested Howles. "I'm a civilian with a federal appointment. I'll make me a formal protest—"

"Really?" said Crook, interrupting. "To whom?"

"Why, to Washington, of course," said Howles. "Maybe they'll send us General Miles. He knows how to deal with Indians."

"You do that, Mr. Howles," said Crook. "Maybe they will send you the general. He's an old friend of mine. But until then, I'll deal with the Apaches my way—and with you and others like you."

"You saw to it the government gave them Turkey Creek," said Howles, beginning to shout, causing his face to turn a darker red. He shook an accusing finger at Crook. "That's good land out there. Too good for Indians. It ought to be homesteaded out. Christ. You didn't even take their guns away."

Crook looked at the man for a moment with disgust. Then he heaved a loud and heavy sigh. "I wonder what the Apaches have done," he said, "to deserve men like you." He turned toward his aide-de-camp. "Mr. Howard," he said, "see to it that Mr. Howles is escorted out of the compound."

Howard gave a nod to Sergeant Mulrey who put a hand on Howles's arm. Howles was furious, but he turned and allowed himself to be led away. There was nothing else he could do. Crook, watching him depart, slowly and sadly shook his head. He was tired, and it was beginning to tell.

Eighty Apaches were gathered on Cibecue Creek listening to the song of a medicine man, when they saw across the creek the red cavalry guidon appear from behind a low hill. The first rider to loom into their view was Dead Shot, wearing his tall white hat. Behind him came thirty troopers and six Apache scouts. Captain Hentig was riding at the head of the troops with Sieber riding beside him.

As the troopers approached the creek, the column fanned out to either side, forming a line which faced the Apaches across the creek. The Apaches turned toward the soldiers, and all of their voices joined with that of the medicine man, their words directed at the cavalry. It made Hentig nervous. What did the words mean? What were they planning to do? Hentig had never seen an Apache war dance. He wondered if this was one.

Nock-ay-del-klinne, or the Dreamer, the leader of the singing, looked at the soldiers and watched them form their skirmish line across the creek. He stared harder at them as he sang louder. He wore a buckskin war shirt, fringed, beaded, and decorated with German silver conchos. His legs were bare, but his lower body was covered by a long and full breechcloth. He wore painted moccasins on his feet, and on his head a leather war cap, decorated with several feathers of the bald eagle. In his right hand, he carried a wand made of flat painted sticks tied together in the form of a cross, and in his left a gourd rattle.

As the skirmish line across the creek settled in place, the voices of the singers died down. A few Apache men ran to their wickieups, only to emerge a moment later armed with carbines or revolvers. Captain Hentig tensed and leaned forward in his saddle to address the crowd across the creek, which was, in his mind, an unruly mob.

"I'm here by order of General Crook," he shouted. "Nantan Lupan. Listen to me."

Hentig spurred his horse to ride into the creek. Sieber and Dead Shot followed his lead, riding one on either side of the captain. They stopped near the other side, still in the water, not far from where Geronimo and the Dreamer stood waiting.

The Dreamer suddenly waded into the creek, splashing and shouted out in Apache.

"The dead chiefs will not rise because there are too many White-eyes on the land," the Dreamer said. "The White-eyes must leave Apache country. I pray that this will happen."

Hentig looked at the Apaches lined up behind Geronimo and the Dreamer. More guns had appeared, some from under blankets. Hentig's horse pranced in the water, and he struggled to keep it under control. The situation did not look good to Hentig. He was afraid that if he didn't say something right away and in the right words, it might get totally out of hand.

"I want those guns put away," he said. "You're allowed firearms for hunting only. Put those rifles away. Now."

He looked back over his shoulder and waved an arm. Five troopers broke out of the skirmish line and rode into the water, crossing the creek and coming to a halt near Sieber, Hentig, and Dead Shot. They held their rifles ready.

"This dance is a demonstration," Hentig proclaimed in a loud voice, "hostile to the citizens of the United States. You are unlawfully assembled. I order you to stop this instant."

He looked down at the Dreamer, who met his gaze for a moment, then suddenly broke into song again. He danced over close to Hentig's horse as he sang, and the charger began to prance and nicker nervously.

"Stop that!" shouted Hentig. "Stop him. Arrest that man."

The Dreamer continued his song and dance, seemingly oblivious to the soldiers around him and to the nervous orders of the captain. A trooper, one of the five who had crossed the creek, loosed a lariat from his saddle. He paid it out, swung it once over his head, and threw a loop, catching the Dreamer, pulling the rope tight and pulling the Dreamer off his feet and down into the water.

The Dreamer clutched at the rope, trying to pull it loose, as he struggled to get back up on his feet, gasping for breath, thrashing about in the water. Sieber drew his revolver and rode toward the medicine man.

"He's not done nothing!" Geronimo shouted in desperation. "We're not bothering no one. You leave here. Leave us alone."

As the Dreamer managed to get to his feet, Sieber leaned over, and with a downward stroke, caught him on the side of the head, knocking him back off his feet and into the water. The Dreamer went under for an instant, then came back up sputtering and spitting water. There was blood on the side of his head, and he held a fist-sized rock which he had picked up from the creek bed in his right hand.

"Watch it!" cried Hentig.

A trooper raised his rifle, took quick aim, and pulled the trigger. The blast shattered the air, and a blotch of dark red suddenly stained the buckskin war shirt of the Dreamer. He stiffened, then fell forward with a final splash into the water. The lower part of his body sank to the bottom of the creek, but his head, shoulders, and upper arms floated on top of the water, bobbing with the current and with the ripples of disturbance from the human and animal activity.

"Shit!" shouted Sieber. "You didn't have to shoot him. I could have handled this whole thing. That's why they pay me."

The Dreamer continued to float facedown in the shallow water, a plume of red blood drifting away across the ripples. His dead right hand still clutched the rock he had picked up from the creek bed.

"What's he got there in his hand?" asked Hentig.

Geronimo waded into the creek and stopped beside the body of the Dreamer. He leaned over and lifted the hand.

"He had a rock," said Hentig. "That's all. A rock."

Geronimo took the rock from the dead man's hand. Then he straightened up and turned to face Dead Shot there beside Hentig. He held out the rock at arm's length toward the scout, balancing it in his open palm.

"They killed him," he said, speaking in Apache, "for this, a piece of the earth."

Nervous and frightened, afraid that he had made a mess of his assignment, Hentig wheeled his horse around, shouting out his desperate orders to the whole of his command.

"Arrest him," he said. "Arrest Geronimo."

Geronimo stood calm, still holding out the rock, still staring at Dead Shot. Dead Shot looked back at Hentig, who seemed to have lost control, not only of the situation, but also of himself. Dead Shot felt trapped. He was a loyal scout in the United States Army, loyal to Nantan Lupan, but he did not like what he had just seen. He looked back at Geronimo who was still standing there in the water holding the rock, still staring at him.

"Whose side are you on?" asked Geronimo, still speaking in his native tongue.

Dead Shot made a quick decision. He pulled his revolver, cocked it, and swung around in his saddle. He aimed and fired, and the bullet ripped through Hentig's head, spraying blood and brains. Hentig's body dropped into the creek.

Sieber spurred his horse and raced toward Geronimo, as the troops on the other side of the creek rode forward. It seemed as if everyone started shooting at once. Apaches fired at the troopers, and the troopers fired at Apaches. The air was filled with the deafening roar of gunshots and the acrid smell of burnt powder. Men shouted. Women screamed in the background, running to find their children.

Geronimo managed to avoid Sieber's rush. He ran through the water and wrenched a revolver from the hand of a mounted trooper. Turning the weapon around in his hand and cocking it, he kept running. He paused beside another mounted trooper long enough to point and fire, sending a bullet into the trooper's face. Not waiting for it to fall, Geronimo dragged the body from the saddle, then jumped onto the horse's back.

Sieber, still intent on Geronimo, turned to pursue him, but an Apache near the wickieups raised his rifle and fired. Sieber felt the bullet tear into his flesh and smash his collar bone, and he screamed out in anger and from the pain and shock, and fell off his horse, landing in the already bloody creek.

Riderless horses ran in confused circles, neighing their fright. Unarmed Apaches ran for cover. Armed Apaches fired at troopers. The troopers, undisciplined without their commanding officer, fired wildly. Women and children ran screaming and crying.

Geronimo, from a distance, mounted on the dead soldier's horse, looked back in horror at the carnage. Several other Apaches had gotten horses and raced to join him. He turned and jumped the cavalry horse over a rock wall, galloping away.

Sieber had dragged himself out of the water, and he saw Geronimo fleeing the scene. He raised his revolver for a long shot and fired. He had meant to shoot Geronimo. The shot went wide and hit another of the fleeing Apaches in the back. The fleeing Indian rode on a little ways before he slipped from the saddle to land hard on the rocky soil.

"Damn," said Sieber. "Damn it to hell. The general ain't going to like this one damn bit."

Chapter 8

In the Great Hall of the Governor's Mansion in Tucson, Arizona Territory, the governor's formal Military Ball was in full swing. A five-piece orchestra was playing a quatrain. Military men in their dress uniforms and civilian men in their finest suits were executing dignified bows and turns with ladies of all ages in lovely evening attire.

General Crook stood beside the punch bowl surrounded by a small crowd of admiring civilians. He was engaged in conversation primarily with an attractive woman of about forty years. Gatewood was standing with a small group of officers off to one side of the room.

Lieutenant Davis was out on the floor performing the stately movements of the quatrain with a very pretty young woman. The sounds of the orchestra, the smells of soap and perfume and powder, the dazzling sight of the Great Hall and the costumes, the tender touch of his partner, and, most of all, the sharp contrast to life at Turkey Creek with the Apaches all combined to make his head swim.

Outside, two sentries stood guard, one on either side of a massive pair of solid, wooden double doors. Their quiet was suddenly disturbed by the sound of rapidly approaching hoof beats. Both sentries stood alert, and in another moment, a military courier rode hard and fast up to the porch, at the last moment, jerking back on the reins, his horse's hoofs scattering gravel around him. He dismounted quickly and mounted the stairway, two and three steps at a time. As he approached the big double doors, one of the sentries, his rifle held across his chest, stepped out to block his way.

"I'm sorry," he said. "Only officers and invited guests are allowed inside."

"Military courier," said the new arrival. "I have an urgent message for the general."

He held out a paper and the sentry moved aside. The courier opened the big door and stepped inside. He stood there only long enough to look quickly around the hall and locate General Crook there beside the punch bowl.

Then he headed directly for Crook, taking long strides right through the middle of the quatrain. The general saw him coming.

"Excuse me," he said to the lady, and he stepped out to meet the courier well away from earshot of those back near the punch bowl. He held out his hand and the courier gave him the paper. Crook opened it and read the message, and a dark cloud seemed to come across his face.

"Thank you," he said. "That's all."

The courier saluted and left the hall. Crook caught the eye of Gatewood and summoned him over.

"Get Lieutenant Davis," he said. Then he led the two junior officers over to a far corner of the room.

"Geronimo's left the reservation," he said, "with about two hundred Chiricahuas. There was a fight at Cibecue. The medicine man was killed there. We lost Captain Hentig, and Al Sieber was wounded."

"Sir?" said Davis.

"Yes, Mr. Davis?"

"I left four men at Turkey Creek."

"They're all dead, Mr. Davis," said the general. "Now there's no need to excite this crowd. Spread the word among the men, quietly. Get them all ready to leave."

"Yes, sir," said Davis. He turned to carry out the command.

"We should make San Carlos by dawn," said Crook to Gatewood. "We'll both take columns south. You follow the river. I'll go by way of Black Mountain. Pursue the murdering bastard and every Apache with him."

"What about the border, sir?" asked Gatewood.

"You hunt him down," said Crook. "Whatever it takes."

A cavalry column accompanied by Apache scouts and leading a pack train of mules snaked its way through the desert. Some distance ahead, Chato and Sergeant Turkey looked for sign. Chato spotted something in the distance and pointed, then spurred his horse. Sergeant Turkey followed close behind.

At the head of the column of soldiers, Gatewood squinted against the desert brightness, watching the two scouts. He could tell that they'd seen something. Then he saw a sudden flash of light, and he knew at once that it was the scouts' signal, sunlight glinting off the polished steel blade of a big bowie knife. He turned in his saddle.

"Gallop the column, Mr. Davis," he said. Then, not waiting, he spurred his own mount, racing ahead toward where Chato and Sergeant Turkey waited. Davis watched him go for a moment. He raised his arm.

"Column at a gallop!" he shouted. "Ho!"

Gatewood reached Chato and reined in his mount with the rest of the column still coming up from his rear. He saw Chato and Sergeant Turkey standing beside their horses. They were looking at something on the ground, and even though he was not yet close enough to tell for sure, Gatewood thought he knew what they had found.

He slowed his mount to a trot and rode in closer, and then he saw the bloody bodies of two men and two mules. All four bodies appeared to have been butchered. Gatewood stayed in the saddle and waited for the column to arrive. When it did, Davis halted it a little ways back, then rode up to stop beside Gatewood. Looking at the scene there before him, Davis paled.

"Couple of prospectors," said Gatewood. "The warriors tied them up. Then the Apache women cut them to ribbons with their knives. One slash at a time."

Davis wanted to look away, but he couldn't. He stared at the horribly mutilated bodies with an ashen face, and he felt as if he could easily become ill and puke or faint or both. He knew that he couldn't afford to let that happen. He fought back the feeling as best he could.

"Ordinarily they'd just kill them," Gatewood continued. "Unless it gets personal. They must have found some scalps or something on those two to make them do this. 'Course the mules were butchered to eat." He turned toward Chato. "How long ago?" he asked.

Chato turned to Sergeant Turkey and spoke briefly in Apache, and the sergeant scout answered. Chato turned back toward Gatewood and spoke in English.

"Two days," he said. "Maybe three. Geronimo break his people into many parts. Small groups. Maybe he do this. Maybe someone else."

Gatewood looked at Davis and noticed the sickly expression on his face. He knew the feeling, and he wondered if he should be thankful that he himself had become used to such sights. It was an awful thing to think that one had become immune to such a thing, but he didn't have time to take pity on Davis's queasy stomach, and even if he had the time, going easy on him would not have done Davis any good. He pretended not to notice.

"You're in charge of the burial, Mr. Davis," he

said. "Have some of the scouts dig a common shallow grave. While you're at it, check for any identification you might find on the bodies or in the packs."

Davis swung down out of the saddle, glad to feel solid ground under his feet. He took a deep breath. Gatewood moved back to the column and got it moving again, leaving Davis there with the Apache scouts. Davis whirled on Chato and spoke with a hard-edged voice.

"Did you kill men like this?" he said, and though he phrased a question, his voice carried an accusatory tone.

"Many times White-eyes do these same things to Apaches," said the scout, his voice calm. "They kill our women. Kill our children. Babies even."

Davis made no response. He continued to stare at Chato with disbelieving and blaming eyes. The Apache scout seemed to have no emotion. He seemed unaffected by the grisly sight there before his eyes.

"Geronimo and the others leave Turkey Creek because of the Dreamer," said Chato, diplomatically changing the subject, "but soon or later, Geronimo would go off anyhow. He's too long away from fighting. He's bad for his people. He's a bad Apache."

In another part of the desert, a column of troopers led by Crook and Sieber came across a lone old Apache woman sitting on the ground, rocking back and forth and singing in a quiet, high-pitched, nasal tone. Crook called a halt to the column. He looked at the woman up ahead. Then he looked questioningly at Sieber.

"It's a death song," said Sieber. "She stayed behind to die."

"They just abandoned her like that?" said Crook.

"It was her own choice," said Sieber. "She didn't want to slow them down no more."

Amazed, Crook stared at the old woman for a long moment before speaking again. "Keep the column moving, Mr. Ragsdale," he said.

Sergeant Ragsdale waved an arm. "Column. Forward. Ho."

Crook urged his mule on, and Sieber kept along beside him. The column moved on slowly, riding past the old woman. The old woman continued her song, continued rocking slowly, ignoring this rude intrusion into her privacy. For all her appearance, in spite of their numbers and the noise they made, she might not have even known they were there.

"They're a tough people, General," said Sieber. "They have to be to survive in this damned country."

Crook muttered something unintelligible as he continued to ride straight ahead. A tough people, he thought. What a perfectly simple-sounding explanation for such a profound experience. He looked back over his shoulder and saw the last of the column passing the old woman. She was merely a small and insignificant dot in the desert in his vision.

The small group of silver miners had been caught by surprise. There had been no chance for them to run for their guns. Almost before they knew what was happening, they had found themselves surrounded by mounted, armed Apaches and herded into a small, tight group. The Apache warriors had formed a circle around the miners and then closed it up tight. There was no escape. The grim-faced warriors sat on their horses and held their rifles pointed down at the helpless and frightened miners.

The miners' faces, all but one, reflected wide-eyed horror at the nearness of almost certain death, at the utter hopelessness of their situation, and at the unknown and therefore wildly imagined manner of their coming executions. The exception, however, was defiant. Then a couple of the mounted Apaches worked their horses sideways, away from each other, their horses bumping into those of their comrades on either side, tightening the circle even more, to make room for another to come riding through.

It was Geronimo. He made his way through the circle of warriors and stopped close to and facing the huddled, frightened miners. He sat straight on the back of the white horse, and he held a Winchester rifle casually in his right hand. He looked down at the miners and studied them in silence for a moment.

"This is Apache land," he said at last. "It has always been Apache land."

"You ain't going to shoot us, are you?" whimpered a miner, taking a timid step forward. "We ain't never done nothing to you. Please. Let us go.

We'll get out of here. We won't come back. I promise."

The defiant one, eyes blazing, turned and roughly shoved the whimpering one back into the crowd, almost knocking him over. Only the bodies of his companions, tightly pressed together, kept him from falling over backward.

"Don't blubber, damn you," said the bold one. "Don't beg the son of a bitch. They're going to kill us all anyway." He turned to face Geronimo. "We make things out of this country," he said. "There was nothing here before we came, and there'd be nothing again if we was to leave it all to you.

"You red son of a bitch. You can kill us, but you're never going to whip us, and I ain't never going to crawl, not to you or any other God-damned Indian."

With no warning, Geronimo leveled his Winchester and fired, the bullet whistling past the ear of the boastful miner and ripping through the skull of one standing just behind him. Blood and brains flew onto the faces of the victim's companions.

"Oh, God!" shouted one.

"No! No!" they cried out, but they did not cry out for long. Geronimo cranked another cartridge into the chamber and fired again, and then the other warriors began to follow his example. There was no fight. It was like shooting ducks in a pond.

Though he flinched at the sound of each shot, in spite of himself, the bold miner stood his ground. The rapid firing around him caused a loud ringing in his ears, but it could not drown out the screams of his fellow miners as Apache bullets tore into their flesh. He clenched his fists at his side, tightened his jaws and stared straight ahead at Geronimo, but out of the corners of his eyes he saw the bodies fall, saw the blood splatter. He waited for the bullet that would rip into his own body and end his life. But it never came.

Suddenly, it was over, and he was still standing, still unhurt. What kind of terrible, slow death had the Apaches saved for him? He wondered if he would be able to hold up to it and die bravely. He swore to himself that he would try, that he would not let the bastards break him, make him scream or cry for mercy.

Geronimo urged his horse forward, riding up very close to the man, and he looked down into the still defiant eyes. "You're a fool," he said. "But at least you're brave. Not like these others. Get off Apache land. The next time I see you, I will kill you."

He jerked his horse around and kicked it in the sides. As Geronimo rode off, the others followed him, taking the miners' horses and mules, leaving the lone, bold miner standing there before a pile of bloody corpses in front of a silver mine there in the Dragoon Mountains.

He had braved the harsh country and the Apaches in a desperate bid for riches. It didn't seem fair. America was supposed to be the land where a man could strike out on his own and go anywhere, take free land, dig in the earth for riches. A poor man could come to this country and become wealthy. The whole world knew the story.

Why had it not worked for him? For these others lying dead around him? What was wrong? Why wasn't the army doing its job? He had silver back in his tent. So had the others. He could take it all now, but he wouldn't be able to carry it. Now he would be lucky to find his way back to civilization alive.

Chapter 9

Gatewood, with Davis riding beside him, was still leading his dusty and weary column along the river, following the orders Crook had given him back at the Governor's Mansion. The column was moving slowly, and Gatewood, his map case on the pommel of his saddle, studied his map, trying to keep himself oriented by checking map points against landscape features. So far, they had seen no Apaches. They had not even seen any sign of Apaches. Then Gatewood looked up, suddenly uneasy. There was no reason, just an undefinable feeling.

"Sergeant Mulrey," he said, keeping his voice down, "send skirmishers out on the point and have them circle back off the trail. Apaches are out there—close by."

"Yes, sir," said Mulrey, riding out of the column. "On the point. Circle back," the sergeant said to some troopers up near the front. As they moved out, he looked anxiously around for any sign that Gatewood knew what he was talking about. He saw none, but he had served long enough with Gatewood to trust the lieutenant's instincts. If Gatewood said there were Apaches out there, then there were Apaches out there as far as Mulrey was concerned.

In the meantime, Gatewood had put away his map to watch the three riders move out on point and turn their mounts to face about. Then he saw on his right flank, atop a nearby ridge, riding along on horseback at an easy pace, fifteen Apache men moving more or less parallel to the column of soldiers.

Davis saw them about the same time, and he turned in his saddle to address Gatewood. "Begging your pardon, sir," he said. "Up there on the ridge—"

"I see them, Mr. Davis," said Gatewood.

"Do we attack?" asked Davis.

"Hold the column steady," said Gatewood, his voice low and calm. Then, turning and raising his voice a little, he said, "Sergeant."

"Steady in the rank," said Mulrey. "Steady."

In low, even voices, troopers passed along the word from one to another all the way down the line.

"Steady in the rank."

"Steady."

"Steady in the ranks."

Gatewood looked up again at the Apaches on the ridge. They still moved slowly, still parallel to the column of soldiers. They did not give any sign that they had even seen the troopers, but Gatewood knew, of course, that they had. He saw no women, no children, no old men, no one on foot. All were young men, well-mounted and well-armed.

"My guess is," he said, "that some young warrior is going to come out—"

He stopped talking as a young Apache, as if to verify Gatewood's surmise, suddenly wheeled his mount to peel off from the group and ride down the steep embankment, heading straight for the approaching column. About fifty yards ahead, down on the flat, he halted his mount. Then he raised his right fist over his head and shouted.

"He's looking for me," said Gatewood. He lifted his own arm to call a halt to the column. "Sergeant Mulrey," he said.

"Column, halt," called out Mulrey.

The column of soldiers stopped moving, and an ominous silence hung heavily in the still desert air. Now and then horses blew, snorted, or pawed at the dusty ground. Up ahead, the lone young Apache warrior sat tall and proud on his horse and stared defiantly at the soldiers. Then he shattered the tense silence by shouting out something in the Apache language. Continuing to shout, he began to prance his horse up and down while delivering his harangue.

"Sir," said Davis, "what do you think he's saying?"

"Insults and challenges," said Gatewood. "As I

suspected, they're meant for me. Hold steady, Mr. Davis."

Davis noticed that the young Apache's face was painted for war with a yellow stripe. He wore a bandanna around his head to hold his long hair in place, a breechcloth, and tall moccasins—nothing else except the ammunition belt around his waist, from which depended an army Colt revolver in a holster. Gatewood turned to Davis.

"Whatever happens here," he said, "the Apaches up on the ridge will all take off. Do not allow the column to pursue at speed. It could be an ambush. Remember this, Mr. Davis. Whenever you can, choose your own ground to fight on."

Then without warning and without any further words of explanation, Gatewood spurred his horse, galloping alone toward the awaiting warrior. Confused, Davis looked around.

"Chato," he said, "what the hell is going on here?"

"This raiding party split off from Geronimo," said Chato. "This Apache has challenged Gatewood to come out and fight. He shows off his power for the other Apaches. He's very young."

Davis looked ahead again. He saw Gatewood ride to within thirty yards of the Apache and stop. The young Apache sat still and quiet for a moment. Then he shouted something else. He pulled out his big Colt Dragoon revolver, yelled, kicked his horse in the sides and headed straight for Gatewood.

Gatewood held his brown cavalry charger steady. Do something, Davis thought, wanting to shout. *Do something.* The Apache, riding hard, fired and missed. It was a long shot for a revolver. Gatewood remained still. Davis, holding his breath and feeling his own heart pounding in his chest, wondered what the hell Gatewood thought he was doing. The Apache would be on top of him in a matter of seconds.

The Apache fired again, and his bullet kicked up dust a few feet to the left of Gatewood's horse. Then, in a sudden and smoothly executed maneuver, one which Davis recognized from the cavalry drill, Gatewood swung out of the saddle, laying his horse over on its side. In the same motion, he slid his Winchester out of its scabbard. The Apache was close, bearing down on him, his revolver leveled for another shot. Gatewood took calm and careful aim and fired.

The sound of the shot shattered the still of the hot, dry desert air. The Winchester bucked in Gatewood's hands, and a blotch of red appeared on the young warrior's chest. He jerked and clutched at the reins of his horse, and the animal veered at the last second to avoid running into Gatewood and his downed charger. The turn was too sharp, and it lost its footing, falling over on its side and throwing its rider, who landed a few feet away with a dull thud, sending up a cloud of dust. Neighing its confusion and fright, the horse got back to its feet to run in bewildered circles. The young warrior did not move.

Gatewood stood looking over at the fallen Apache for a moment. Then he turned to look at the others still up on the ridge, and he saw them whip their mounts up to a gallop and ride away, disappearing on the other side of the ridge. Davis hurried out to Gatewood's side.

"Are you all right, sir?" he asked.

"I'm fine, Mr. Davis," said Gatewood. He got his horse to its feet and returned the rifle to its scabbard.

Davis dismounted and walked over for a closer look at the fallen Apache. "He's dead, sir," he said. "I knew him at Turkey Creek. He's only about seventeen years old. Younger than I am."

"Let's get the column moving, Mr. Davis," said Gatewood. "We're back to tracking."

Davis swallowed hard. "Yes, sir," he said, and he turned his horse to ride back to the column.

Outside the door of the stockade at San Carlos, a mounted corporal sat stiffly in the saddle on guard duty. A short distance away, on the parade ground, one hundred smartly dressed infantry soldiers stood with rifles at parade rest, and one hundred mounted troopers held their chargers still in formation. Civilians stood around in front of the buildings, and a small crowd had gathered below and in front of a newly constructed gallows from which dangled three nooses. A heavy and ominous silence seemed to hang in the air.

The door to the stockade opened from the inside, and a burly first sergeant stepped out to stand beside the door and bark out a call to attention. One hundred mounted cavalrymen and one hundred infantrymen all snapped to at once. The grim faces of the troopers stared straight ahead, but their eyes all looked toward the stockade as three Apache prisoners and their military escort emerged.

The solemn escort led the Apaches to the gallows and up the steps, placing them carefully on the trapdoor. All eyes, military and civilian, white, Indian, and Mexican, male and female, young and old, watched. All faces were grim. A corporal knelt to tie the prisoners' feet, as General Crook, accompanied by a chaplain, mounted the scaffold. The corporal, finished with his job, stood up and stepped back to prepare more bindings for the hands and arms.

Crook turned to face the assembly, and, almost at once, he saw in the small crowd gathered there below the gibbet, the beautiful young wife of Dead Shot. Her eyes seemed to look straight into his own, accusing, hating, pleading, threatening, all at once. He felt his own gaze pulled to hers, held captive, by some force he could not control. At last he managed to tear himself away. He drew himself up to his tallest height and took a deep breath. Then he unfolded a paper from which to read.

"The Chiricahuas known as Dandy Jim and Skip-Hey," he read, "have been found guilty by the Military Court, Department of Arizona, of insurrection at Cibecue Creek. The Chiricahua Dead Shot, Sergeant, Apache Scouts, Sixth Cavalry, has been found guilty of treason. The sentence of the court for the three prisoners is death by hanging."

Crook folded up the paper and tucked it away inside his jacket. He turned to stand solemn and silent beside the chaplain, facing the three condemned prisoners. He carefully avoided the eyes of Dead Shot, standing there in his tall white top hat.

"Do any of you have anything to say to me as chaplain?" asked the military clergyman, his voice sounding weak and uncertain. "Are any of you Christians?"

There was no response, and the chaplain bowed his head, clutching his Bible in both hands in front of his chest. The three condemned prisoners stood looking straight ahead, their dark faces betraying no emotion. Dead Shot took off his tall white top hat and held it out toward Crook.

"Nantan Lupan," he said, "I give you my hat. It will remind you of my wife and baby."

Crook accepted the hat, feeling a choking sensation in his throat, as the corporal again stepped up close behind the prisoners, this time to bind their arms, and finally, to adjust the nooses, taking care to snug down each knot just above and behind the left ear of each prisoner.

Suddenly Dandy Jim cried out in Apache in a loud and clear voice. "Listen, my relatives," he said. "Don't trust the White-eyes. With them there is no right way."

Apache voices muttered in the crowd, and Dandy Jim abruptly changed to English to conclude the final statement of his life. "To you White-eyes," he said, "I am not afraid of your preacher. The Lifegiver will welcome me."

Down in the crowd below the gibbet, the wife of Dead Shot stood. Tears ran freely down her cheeks. She had tried to control herself, to remain dignified in the face of her husband's death, but the outburst of Dandy Jim broke through her stoicism. She stood trembling and biting her lower lip. Then she could stand it no more. She could no longer hold it inside.

She screamed and produced a knife from underneath her blanket, then rushed forward, trying desperately and foolishly to reach her husband. Two troopers hurried forward, grabbed her by her arms, one on each side, and held her back. For a moment she struggled and shouted. One of the soldiers wrenched the knife from her grasp, and then she gave up all at once and collapsed, sobbing. The two soldiers held her up on her feet, or she would have fallen to the ground. What would she have done had the soldiers not grabbed her in time? Killed Crook? Cut loose her husband? It was a hopeless, futile gesture in the face of a hopeless situation.

With the woman subdued, the chaplain looked nervously over the crowd. Crook cleared his throat loudly. The murmurs of the crowd subsided. Then, again, all was silence.

Suddenly there was the loud clunk of the lever being pulled, followed by the sound of the heavy trapdoors falling, and three men plummeted downward, jerking grotesquely as they reached the ends of the ropes.

It was a good hanging. Their necks were broken, and the Apaches died instantly. The three bodies each made a quarter of a turn to the right, then dangled there in front of the morbidly fascinated crowd, swaying back and forth a little. The ceremony was done.

Chapter 10

Gatewood and his column continued on patrol on the trail of the Apaches they had seen earlier on the ridge. Chato was able to follow the signs easily enough, but the small group of mounted young men was traveling light, moving quickly and staying well ahead of their blue-coated pursuers.

Gatewood had no idea whether or not he was on the trail of Geronimo. He had seen a small group of young Apache men. That's all. They could have been a group that broke away from Geronimo's band. They could even have been a different band altogether. It was possible, however, that they were part of Geronimo's band and would lead Gatewood to a place of rendezvous with the larger band. At any rate, theirs was the only trail he had to follow. And even if they did not eventually lead him to Geronimo, if he could only catch up with them, he would at least be able to return to San Carlos with something to show for his efforts.

It was about noon when Gatewood saw the sight ahead that made him call an unexpected halt to his column. Not far in front of him was a stagecoach, standing ominously stark, still, and noiseless in the middle of the vast desert. The traces were empty, the six-up team having vanished. There was no sign of life, yet there were no bodies in sight either.

"Sergeant Mulrey," said Gatewood, "select three troopers. Follow Lieutenant Davis and me. On the double."

Without waiting for Mulrey and the troopers, Gatewood headed for the coach. Davis stayed right beside him. He was not anxious to see the sight he knew awaited him there. Sergeant Mulrey and three troopers came up soon behind. They all rode over to the stagecoach and dismounted. Gatewood stepped over to the coach and reached for the door handle. He hesitated for an instant, and then he opened the door. The head and arm of a body which had been pressed against the door on the inside fell back to dangle there near enough for Gatewood to touch. Davis, from where he stood back, waiting, could see the bodies inside—and the blood.

"Four of them," said Gatewood. "It looks to me like the Apaches killed them just to get the horses —either to ride or to eat."

"Sir," said Davis. "Was it the same bunch we've been following?"

"Chato?" said Gatewood, glancing toward the scout.

Chato nodded. "Same bunch," he said.

"Sir," said Davis. "Over there."

Gatewood looked back over his shoulder and saw that Davis was pointing toward a dust cloud on the far horizon. Not waiting for orders, troopers were pulling carbines out of their scabbards. Nerves were on edge. Gatewood drew out his field glasses for a better look.

"It's Sieber," he said, lowering the glasses. "Everyone stand easy." He swung back into the saddle and spurred his charger to ride out and meet the chief of scouts. "Come on," he said to the small group there with him at the coach.

Davis and the others remounted and rode hard after Gatewood. When the six soldiers drew near Sieber, who had Sergeant Dutchy, the Apache scout, riding along with him, they hauled back hard on the reins of their mounts, bringing them to a skiddering halt. Sieber and Dutchy stopped their horses, too, and Sieber pulled a piece of paper out from inside his shirt. He held it out at arm's length toward Gatewood. Without a word, Gatewood took the paper and opened it to read.

"The general wants to deploy me and Dutchy to your column," said Sieber. He paused a moment while Gatewood continued reading. Gatewood, still reading the dispatch, made no immediate response.

"How's the wound, Mr. Sieber?" asked Davis. The thought of having a partially disabled man along on patrol worried him.

"Hell, I mend real good," said Sieber. "It ain't slowing me down none. I guarantee you that." He watched as Gatewood folded the dispatch and tucked it into his saddlebag. "The general figures if anybody's going to catch up with old Geronimo," he said to Gatewood, "it's going to be you."

"We just came across an Overland," said Gatewood. "Four passengers dead. Horses gone."

"He's burned two spreads to the west of here," said Sieber. "He's got plenty of horses and food. Picked up ammunition. I figure he'll keep tracking off to the hills."

"We don't really know that it's Geronimo we're tracking," said Gatewood.

"Well, if it ain't," said Sieber, "it's damn sure some of his boys. I can promise you that."

"Mr. Davis," said Gatewood, "Sergeant Mulrey, stick with Mr. Sieber. See that he finds his way back to the column by sundown. Sergeant Roundtree, the column gets twenty minutes. Tobacco and coffee. We have bodies to attend to here."

Sieber spurred his horse. Sergeant Dutchy, Davis, and Mulrey were right behind him. Gatewood stood for a moment watching them go. He hoped they would be all right. They should be, he told himself. Sieber was a man of vast experience.

Sieber and Dutchy rode at a canter slightly ahead of Davis and Mulrey. Suddenly Sieber hauled up and dismounted. He knelt to examine hoof prints in the sand. Dutchy stayed in his saddle nearby.

"The raiding party's close," said Sieber. He looked back toward Mulrey and Davis who had come on up from behind. "You ride for the column, Sarge," he said to Mulrey. "Bring them back here to pick up this trail. Pronto." He shot a glance at Davis. "With your permission, of course, Lieutenant," he added.

Mulrey glanced at Davis, and Davis gave him a nod. Sieber stood up to unboot his Winchester and gave Sergeant Mulrey's horse a whack across the rump. As Mulrey galloped back toward the column, Sieber climbed up again into his saddle.

He took the lead as before, following the trail he had just been studying. Sergeant Dutchy and Lieutenant Davis rode alongside him. Sieber set the pace at a gallop, occasionally slowing down to check the trail. Then he saw up ahead three young Apaches moving along easily with a string of horses. The trailing Apache looked over his shoulder and saw the soldiers coming. He turned back around and yelled out something in Apache to the one in the lead. As they jerked their ponies into a gallop, the third Apache split off to go his own way, taking four of the extra horses with him. Sieber spurred his mount, racing after the main body. He made a wild gesture toward the third Apache, the lone rider.

"Take him," he shouted back at Davis.

Davis and Dutchy raced in pursuit of the third Apache, who had by then become widely separated from the other two. The Apache looked back and saw them coming, saw them gaining on him, and he abandoned his four extra mustangs and raced toward the far horizon at a full gallop, lashing at his pony with a quirt.

Davis and Dutchy continued riding hard for a moment, until Davis realized that the gap between them and the Apache was widening, and he knew that it would be hopeless to continue the chase. He reined in his mount suddenly. Dutchy did the same. Davis hauled out his Springfield carbine and dismounted. He leveled the carbine across his horse's back, using the saddle as a rest. The fleeing Apache looked very small on the horizon. Davis took careful aim. He hesitated.

"Use long gun," said Dutchy.

He held out a Sharps toward Davis, who took it, tossing the carbine back to the scout. He laid the Sharps across his saddle as he had the carbine and sighted in. His target had become nothing more than a dot over his sights. He knew he would have time for only one shot, and he wanted to make it count. Slowly he squeezed the trigger, and there was a resounding boom, as the big gun jerked upward and kicked back into his shoulder.

Dutchy and Davis stared off across the flat, dry landscape, the echo of the shot resounding into the distance. Davis rubbed his shoulder where the gun had kicked it.

"You miss," said Dutchy.

The lone rider on the far horizon was gone in another instant. It was as if no one had ever been there.

* * *

Sieber had raced alone after the other two Apaches, the ones with the main string of horses. Carrying his carbine in his right hand, he used it to lash at his horse. Then, when he had the distance he wanted between him and his target, he made a running dismount, shouldered the carbine and fired. His shot went wide, and he fired again. After the second shot, he could see the trailing Apache give a jerk, slump forward, then fall sideways off his horse.

The lead Apache, alone now, heard the shots, and he wheeled his horse to face Sieber. The string of captured horses, suddenly free of any control, and hearing shots fired, began to buck and rear and neigh their protests. The Apache raised his rifle as Sieber, remounted, galloped forward.

The two riders were about fifty yards apart when the Apache fired. Sieber knew that his horse was hit when he felt it dropping out from under him. He flung himself from the saddle as the horse collapsed, nose first, and rolled. Sieber rolled too, into a tangle of brush.

The Apache kept riding forward, firing at the brush where he had seen Sieber disappear. Sieber scrambled over to the dead horse, keeping low behind its body. The Apache, still riding hard, fired two more shots, both slamming into the dead horse.

Then, with the Apache no more than twenty yards away, Sieber suddenly popped up from behind the body of his mount, his rifle raised. He fired, and the Apache's head jerked, a splotch of red appearing on his forehead. Sieber fired again, unnecessarily, and hit the chest. The warrior flipped backward off the running horse to land hard in the hot desert sand, momentarily stirring up a cloud of dust. The confused horse continued running forward a few paces, slowed, turned, and trotted off in another direction. The cloud of dust around the fallen warrior settled, and the air was still again.

Sergeant Mulrey was leading the column back to where he had left Sieber, Davis, and Dutchy. The column had already picked up Davis and the scout sergeant, and they moved on in the direction Dutchy told them Sieber had gone in pursuit of the two Apaches with the string of horses. Mulrey pointed ahead.

"There, Lieutenant," he said.

Gatewood looked and saw Sieber up ahead, sitting on the rump of a dead horse. He urged the column forward, but at an easy trot. It was obvious that the chief of scouts was in no trouble. Whatever had happened was over and done. Coming closer, Gatewood saw that Sieber was casually cleaning his carbine. Gatewood halted the column, then rode ahead with Davis, Mulrey, and Dutchy, bringing them to a halt up close to Sieber.

"Everything all right here, Mr. Sieber?" he asked.

Sieber looked around as if to make sure before answering Gatewood's question. "Yeah. Looks like it," he said. "We caught up with three bucks running a string of stolen ponies. I gave one of them to Mr. Davis there, but it seems like that one got away."

Davis felt the sting of the scout's comment, but he kept silent. Sieber stood up and turned to look at the dead horse upon which he had been sitting. Gatewood glanced back at Davis, then looked at the dead Apache, lying in the sand not twenty yards away.

"The other one's on out there," said Sieber, with a jerk of his head.

"Sergeant Mulrey," said Gatewood, "check over there for signs of a dead hostile."

Mulrey spurred his mount and rode in the direction Sieber had indicated.

"When these two bucks here don't show up for dinner this evening," said Sieber, stretching, "old Geronimo's going to be across that border damn fast."

He looked up at Gatewood for some kind of response to his observation, but he received none.

"We cross into Mexico tomorrow?" Sieber asked.

"That's right, Mr. Sieber," said Gatewood.

"Well, I'd say we ought to send some of the scouts back to San Carlos," said Sieber. "I don't trust them down south of the border. Geronimo's got a couple of them spooked already. They're starting to wonder if they might not be fighting on the wrong side."

"I don't think so, Mr. Sieber," said Gatewood. "We need every scout we have."

"You wouldn't say that if you'd been there when Dead Shot and the rest of them turned on us at Cibecue," said Sieber, suddenly losing his patience with the officer.

"On the contrary, Mr. Sieber," said Gatewood,

"if I'd been at Cibecue, they wouldn't have turned. The whole thing wouldn't have happened."

Before Sieber had a chance to respond to the not too subtle accusatory tone of Gatewood's voice, Sergeant Mulrey shouted from off in the distance.

"He's here," he called out. "You got him clean, Mr. Sieber."

That announcement was followed by a moment of tense silence. Sieber glanced out toward Mulrey, then looked back at Gatewood.

"I know you don't like me much, Lieutenant," Sieber said. "I guess because I'm a little rough in my ways. I ain't the gentleman type. But at least compared to you, I'm honest."

"What's that supposed to mean, Mr. Sieber?" asked the lieutenant.

"No offense intended, Mr. Gatewood, and speaking off the record, sir, I figure you're a real sad case. You don't love who you're fighting for, and you don't hate who you're fighting against."

Gatewood returned Sieber's hard stare for another tense moment before responding. The desert air was heavy and still, and the silence was broken only by the sounds of Mulrey's horse, as the sergeant rode back from the location of the distant body.

"Maybe I could learn to hate with the proper vigor, Mr. Sieber," said Gatewood, "if I was to spend enough time in your company."

"Maybe you could, Lieutenant," said Sieber, and he stood up and turned to walk away. Gatewood sat still in his saddle and watched.

* * *

High up in the Sierra Madres, in a camp of scattered wickieups, old Nana sat cross-legged on the hard, parched soil in the hastily made camp. They had only just stopped for the night. Geronimo rode up and dismounted. He walked over close to Nana.

"I know you are angry about this war," he said. "The White-eyes gave me no choice. I ask your blessing."

"You ask my blessing," said Nana, "after the thing is done."

"What I did is right," said Geronimo, his voice betraying rising anger.

"They have many guns and we have few," said Nana. "The reservation is bad, but at least we can stay alive."

"In the Blue Mountains the White-eyes will never catch us," said Geronimo.

"Many Apaches will die," said the old man. "I must send for Nantan Lupan. We will talk with him. I ask that you do this."

Geronimo turned away looking north and stared off into the distance. He knew that Nana was a great leader, and, of course, he had great respect for the old man. He had been short with Nana, and he was sorry for that. But he had trusted the White-eyes before. More than once. And he felt himself a fool for having trusted them at all after the first time they had lied to him. He had sworn that he would never trust them again. He recalled the senseless killing of the Dreamer. There had been no reason for that. There could be no explanation. The

White-eyes were crazy—blood crazy and land crazy—and that was all.

He remembered the White-eye scout Sieber telling him that he had no right to leave Turkey Creek. He did not think that he belonged to the White-eyes, that they could tell him where to go and where not to go. White men moved about freely, going where they wanted to go and doing what they wanted to do, even moving onto Apache land without asking for permission. Why then should he, Geronimo, or any other Apache, have to live at the indulgence and according to the whims of the white man?

He knew that Usen, the Lifegiver, had put the Apaches on the earth where he had meant them to be, and he knew that his own mother, after his birth, had rolled him on the ground in the four directions to ensure that he would remain attached to that land and love the land forever.

He also knew that the life of the Apaches had been good before the White-eyes came. They had moved about as they liked, and they had always had plenty to eat. Even when the White-eyes came, the Apaches had welcomed them, and they had showed them that they could get along together, if not like brothers, then certainly as good neighbors.

Geronimo knew well the story of the beginning of the troubles with the White-eyes. It had been started by a white man named Ward who had an Indian wife and a half-breed son. This had been back in the days of Cochise.

One day Ward had beaten his son unmercifully, and the boy had run away to Cochise for safety.

Ward claimed that Cochise had stolen the boy along with some of his livestock. The bluecoats had believed Ward, and Bascom, the soldier chief of that time, had sent word to Cochise that he wanted him to come in for a conference.

Cochise and twelve others had gone to talk with Bascom, but when they got inside his tent, he ordered them arrested. Cochise had reacted quickly. Pulling his knife and slicing through the canvas back of the tent, he had escaped through the opening he made there. But his relatives, those who had gone with him, did not escape, and Bascom had refused to let them go.

Cochise and his warriors then captured three white men and offered to exchange them for the Apaches who were being held by Bascom, but Bascom refused. Cochise ordered the prisoners killed, and, in retaliation, Bascom had the twelve Apaches hanged.

That had all happened when Geronimo was a young man, and he remembered it well. He knew, too, that it had become a pattern, the kind of behavior to be expected from the white men.

He had also learned that when three or four bad white men stopped and robbed a stagecoach, and maybe even killed someone, the white men would send out one sheriff to catch them. But if three or four bad Indians stopped a stage, killed someone, or even stole a cow, the army would come in full force, intent on destroying every Apache they could find.

It was not good, and it was not right. Geronimo hated the White-eyes, he thought, with good reason. He would rather die fighting them than go back to the reservation and probably be put in their stockade, perhaps even be hanged. He would rather die a free man than live on as a slave or be killed like a slave.

But he knew that Mangas was right. Old Nana had to be respected. And he was not the only one. There were others, many of them much younger than Nana, who were tired of the war trail, tired of running and hiding. They missed their families, many of whom were back on the reservation. Yes. Nana's feelings had to be considered.

Chapter 11

General Crook rode across Canyon de los Embudos in Mexico. He rode his favorite army mule and carried his shotgun across his saddle. He was dressed in his favorite white stable clothes, the trousers held up by wide suspenders, and he wore a slouch hat on his head. A small entourage, consisting of a few troopers and Apache scouts, Gatewood, Davis, Sieber, and a civilian photographer named C. S. Fly from Tombstone, accompanied him. As they rode along in the shadows of a deep gulch, silhouetted Chiricahua Apaches stood and walked along the ridge above. The uneasy photographer, his neck craned, studied the ridge with obvious and nervous agitation.

"Look," he said. "Look up there. There's more of them. General?"

"Don't get nervous now, son," said Crook. The general rode straight ahead. He remained calm. He did not even seem to be at all concerned with the Apaches who were watching them from up above.

"They could kill us all," said Fly. "We wouldn't have a chance."

"Why don't you take their picture?" said Crook. "They'd like that." He turned in his saddle to address Sieber. "What do you think, Al?"

"You know damn well what I think, General," said Sieber, failing to see any humor in Crook's remarks. "We win the wars. Geronimo wins the peace. Makes promises he don't intend to keep. It's always the same story."

Crook looked up and around at the surrounding Apaches. "It's only okay when we do it. Right, Al?" he said. "Make promises we don't intend to keep?"

Sieber rode on stony-faced, oblivious to the general's irony, and soon they reached the appointed place of rendezvous. There were no Apaches there waiting for them, but Crook was not concerned. He ordered a camp to be made, and he settled down to wait. Then Geronimo came.

Crook was confident in his position to dictate the terms of surrender, for it had been Geronimo himself who had asked for this meeting. He expected the old warrior to argue and to make demands of his own, but in the end, Crook was certain, he would win.

Geronimo and his small band had lined up in front of Fly's camera, their weapons in their hands. Geronimo wore a red bandanna tied around his head to hold back his hair. He also wore his dark jacket over the spotted shirt. Fly had his head under a black cloth that was draped over his camera, which was mounted on a tripod, and he held a little stick in his hand which had a crosspiece on top of it.

"Come forward a little," Fly said.

Geronimo spoke briefly in Apache, and the warriors all moved forward. They stood with stern expressions on their faces, holding their rifles or revolvers ready. Fly pushed the button, and the powder on top of the stick flashed. The Apaches, all except Geronimo, murmured in awe of the flash.

They sat on the ground in a dry river bottom in the Canyon de los Embudos. Crook smoked his pipe. It was midmorning, and the council was already well underway. The day was hot already. It would get worse before it was over.

"I never do wrong without a cause," Geronimo was saying. "There is one God looking down on us all. We are all children of the one God."

"I didn't come here to listen to you talk about religion," said Crook. "You broke your word. You left Turkey Creek. You killed many White-eyes. Now I want you to come back to San Carlos with me. Then Washington wants you to go to Florida. You do it, or I'll come back with my army and fight."

"I don't know about Florida," said Geronimo.

"It's a long way away," said Crook. "You'll be kept on a special reservation there."

"Nantan Lupan does not understand," said Geronimo, his voice revealing exasperation. "The White-eyes always try to change the Apache way, try to make the Apaches act like White-eyes."

"The Apaches were doing fine growing corn," said Crook. "The problem was Geronimo. I knew Cochise. He was a king. A wise ruler of his people. I knew Victorio. A proud leader. And I know Geronimo. He doesn't want to lead or rule or be wise. He only wants to fight."

Geronimo rankled under this tirade from Crook. Things were not going well. This was what he had been afraid of. Even Nantan Lupan, one of the best of the White-eyes, would not listen to reason. He remembered everything the Apaches had ever done, but he refused to acknowledge even one wrong thing done by white men.

"I didn't start this trouble," Geronimo said, almost sulking. "The army killed the Dreamer. Why? What was he doing wrong? There was no reason to kill him. That was the cause of all this trouble."

"He was calling for war," Crook snapped back. "If the medicine man had come in peaceably, he'd still be alive today. There is no excuse for taking up arms against the United States Army. The army is the best friend the Chiricahuas have, damn it. You know it. I know it."

More lies, thought Geronimo, but he could see no profit in continuing to argue. Nantan Lupan was not listening to what he had to say. It was like talking to a man who could not hear. Geronimo looked around, as if he were looking for the answer to some elusive question.

"I don't understand," Geronimo said. "With all this land, why is there no room for the Apaches? Why do the White-eyes want all the land?"

Crook did not bother trying to answer that question. He knew that there was no answer, and he saw no reason to get into a debate on the issue with Geronimo. Besides, it mattered little what he might think. It made no difference that much of what Geronimo said was true, and that Crook could not give satisfactory answers to the very legitimate questions the Apache asked. Crook's own sense of humanity and justice and right was totally irrelevant. His superiors in Washington were single-minded when it came to Indians. He knew that, too. He stared straight ahead at Geronimo and remained silent.

Geronimo sighed heavily. He looked at Crook. It was obvious that the general had quit talking. The conference was over, and it was now up to Geronimo to make a decision. He knew what he had to do, and he hated it, but he had to think of the others and what they wanted.

"How long in Florida?" he asked.

"Maybe two years," said Crook. "With your families. I think I can get that. It's not a bad deal. There are lots of White-eyes who want to hang Geronimo for murder."

"Not murder," said Geronimo, standing up and beginning to pace angrily. "War. Bad things happen in war. Maybe White-eyes should hang for killing Apaches."

"How many White-eyes have you killed since

you left Turkey Creek?" asked Crook, begging the question.

"I don't know," said Geronimo. "Maybe fifty. Maybe more. How many Apaches did you kill?"

"You killed women and children," accused Crook.

"So did you."

"Are we going to give speeches," said the general, "or are we going to make a deal?"

Geronimo stopped pacing and looked down, but he avoided Crook's eyes. There was a long moment of silence. Then Nana spoke up.

"We gain nothing by fighting," Nana said. "We can live on the reservation. I'll go there. You, Nantan Lupan, are like a father to me."

Crook looked back toward Geronimo, who continued to avoid his gaze. It was clearly Geronimo's move.

"Many of my people want to surrender," Geronimo said, and he sounded tired, if not defeated. "Maybe I'll surrender to you."

He paused and looked off toward the mountains.

"When I was young," Geronimo continued, "the White-eyes came and wanted the land of my people. When the soldiers burned our villages, we moved into the mountains. When they took our food, we ate thorns. When they took our children, we had more." He turned suddenly to face Crook, and with his next words, his voice raised in both volume and intensity. "We killed all the White-eyes we could. We said we would never give up our land, never surrender. We starved, and we killed, but in our heart, we never surrendered. Now—"

"Could you look up, Geronimo?" said Fly from under his black cloth. "Nana, Ulzana, move a little closer. General, this way, please."

All of the parties complied docilely with the photographer's wishes, almost as if they knew they were participants in a historic moment. Fly fired again, causing another flash.

Off to one side at a respectful distance, Gatewood, Davis, and Sieber watched the proceedings. Gatewood seemd agitated. It was clear to Sieber that Gatewood was not pleased with the way things were going, that he did not like seeing Geronimo being brought so close to humiliation. Sieber stepped up close beside Gatewood.

"I wonder," he said, "how many times in my life I get to see Geronimo surrender?"

It was dusk in the canyon when Crook mounted up to ride out. Old Nana and his band, with a number of women and children, rode along with him. Geronimo stood by watching.

As the party moved out, Gatewood rode over close to where Geronimo was standing. "I'm being left behind," he said, "with a few men. When you're ready to start for San Carlos, come on down from your camp. I'll be waiting for you."

"You still want me to be a farmer, Gatewood?" said Geronimo. "I think maybe you like the warrior best, like you—soldier."

The two warriors looked at each other for a moment. Then Gatewood turned his mount and walked it slowly away.

Alone, Geronimo thought about the council with

Crook. He had gone to the meeting expecting to surrender. He had come to that decision because of the feelings of Nana and the others. Not his own feelings. No. Still, he had gone there expecting to give himself up to Nantan Lupan.

But he did not like the way Crook had talked to him, and he did not like the way old Nana had humbled himself before Crook. Nana had been a great leader and a great warrior, and he should not have to behave that way to be allowed to live in peace.

Well, Nana had surrendered, but Geronimo had not. He had only said, "Maybe."

"Gokhlaye."

He turned to see who was calling his name. A young man was running toward him.

"What is it?" Geronimo asked.

"There's been an accident."

Geronimo got up to follow the young man, and they ran back into the village and through it to the other side. There a group of Apaches were standing around with their heads bowed.

"What is it?" asked Geronimo.

"They're drunk," said the young man. He pointed to the steep hillside just a little ways ahead. "That one tried to ride his horse down there. He fell, and he was killed."

Geronimo was furious.

"Where is the whiskey?" he said. "Where did it come from?"

Gatewood waited a week for Geronimo to come down from his camp, before he admitted to himself that it was not going to happen. Geronimo had changed his mind, and Gatewood thought that he knew why. Geronimo had been ready to come in, but Crook had botched it at the end. He had said some wrong things, things that Geronimo simply would not take.

Even so, the whole situation irked Gatewood, for several reasons. He was angry and frustrated that Crook had spoiled the deal. He was angry at Geronimo for setting him up to look like a fool. But most of all he was angry at Al Sieber, for he knew what the scout was thinking: if they had all listened to Sieber in the first place, they wouldn't be in this position now.

He ordered his small party, consisting of Davis, Sieber, Chato, and a few other Apache scouts, to get ready to ride. They moved up into the nearby hills, looking for Geronimo. For once, they didn't have to look far to pick up the trail.

It was almost as if the sign had been left especially for them to find. They came across the body of a man, suspended by his feet from the canyon wall. Sieber estimated that the body had been hanging there for at least three days.

"Buzzards've picked his eyes out," Sieber said. "It looks to me like old Charlie Tribollet. He was probably down here selling whiskey." He paused and smiled, clearly pleased to have himself proved right. "Sure don't look like the work of Mexicans, does it?"

"Chiricahua," said Chato.

"Geronimo," said Gatewood.

Chato nodded in agreement. "Prob'ly so," he

said. "This man sells whiskey to the Indians. The Indians get drunk. Sometimes they do crazy things. Sometimes they fight each other. Maybe even get killed."

"And that's why Geronimo did this?" asked Davis.

Chato shrugged. "Maybe," he said.

"Hell," said Sieber, "he just done it to let us know where he stands. That's all."

Gatewood had some thoughts on the matter, but he kept them to himself. They cut down the body and buried it in a shallow grave. Sieber protested that it was a waste of time and energy, and that Tribollet had been no good in life and so was undeserving of such consideration in death. But Gatewood had insisted. The unpleasant chore done, they rode on.

Mangas and old Nana sat before a wickieup in a scattered camp in the mountains. Geronimo walked over and sat down with them. Nana was singing softly to himself.

"Old Nana and his people," said Mangas, "will return to Turkey Creek. Many of his people are too old to fight."

Geronimo looked at Nana. "Nantan Lupan will make you a prisoner," he said.

The old man stopped singing.

"I have to trust him," he said. "I have no choice. I said he was my brother. But he is an enemy."

"Go if you must," said Geronimo. "I have made my decision. I will not surrender to the White-eyes."

"I'll stay with you and fight," said Mangas. "But now we will be very few."

Farther on, atop a high mesa, Chato, on foot, stared off at the desert a thousand feet below. Beyond the desert loomed another mountain range, purple in the distance.

"The trail goes off here," said Chato. "He's down there in the desert. Maybe two days ahead."

He turned to face the others, all still mounted. Then he pointed off across the flats to the far mountain range.

"Geronimo's going to be in those mountains tomorrow," Chato said.

"What happened?" said Davis. "I thought he was coming in."

Chato shrugged. "He changed his mind," he said. "He's a bad Apache."

Gatewood knew what had happened, but he kept it to himself. He would not blame a superior officer openly and in front of others. Besides, it would do no good to say anything more. What was done was done. He looked over at Sieber, and found the scout already looking at him.

"Say it, Mr. Sieber," said Gatewood. "You were right."

"I ain't one to rub it in, Lieutenant," said Sieber, "but it is going to be hell to pay. That son of a bitch Geronimo has took advantage of the general's better nature."

He turned his head to spit a fine spray of amber from the chaw in his right cheek. Gatewood looked forward again and stared out at the desert for a long, uncomfortable moment.

"Sir," said Davis, "hadn't we best report Geronimo's flight to General Crook? The closest heliograph sentry is at Burning Rock."

"Lead the way, Mr. Davis," said Gatewood, and Davis could not help but think that Gatewood seemed like a defeated man. He hesitated only a moment, then turned his horse, leading the others away. Gatewood, though, did not move. He sat still in his saddle and continued to stare out at the vast desert below and beyond.

Chapter 12

They returned to San Carlos without Geronimo, but their rest was short. Crook sent them out again, this time with Gatewood in command of a large force and with clear orders to pursue Geronimo as far into Mexico as necessary.

"Just get him," Crook had said.

Early the next morning, Gatewood's column crossed the border into Mexico, and for six long weeks, they tracked through Sonora and into the Sierra Madre Mountains. Suffering long, forced marches with dwindling food supplies, they searched out known haunts of Geronimo, following the lead of Sieber and of the Apache scouts. They checked rumors and reports, and they continued their hunt. There was no sign of Geronimo.

It was dusk, and the column had camped for the

night. Small campfires burned here and there throughout the bivouac. The troopers were eating their meager evening meal of coffee and hardtack. There was much quiet grumbling around the fires. The soldiers were tired and sore. They were sick of what seemed to them to be nothing more than a wild goose chase. They needed baths and a good meal and a good night's rest in real beds. Sieber sat with Davis outside the door of the lieutenant's tent. A small fire burned in front of them.

During the long campaign, Davis had gradually learned to get along with the crusty chief of scouts. He saw Sieber, finally, not as a friend, but as a man of vast knowledge gained from years of experience. Only a fool, he thought, would not try to profit from association with the man. Sieber seemed to love talking about the Apaches, and in his own way, Davis thought, he was as taken by them as was Lieutenant Gatewood.

It was the man's hard edge that made him seem such a puzzle. Davis wondered if it was simply a result of the life Sieber led, this life in the Arizona Territory chasing Apaches. Then he realized that Lieutenant Gatewood also had that hard edge, although he was much more polished than Sieber. And he wondered if he would acquire it himself, if he kept at this work long enough. He found the thought a little frightening. He wasn't at all sure that he wanted that hard edge.

"Well, sir," Sieber was saying, "your Apache rides one horse plumb to death, then eats him and steals another one. A horse is mobile food to him.

That's all. I've chased Apaches who've made fifty miles a day on horseback and on foot."

"Fifty miles a day?" said Davis, incredulous. He forced himself to take another bite of hardtack, thinking that perhaps they would have a little beef again in the morning. He hoped so.

"You damn right," said Sieber. He slurped some hot coffee from a tin cup. "Sometimes seventy. Hell, they can live on cactus. Go forty-eight hours without water. One week of that'll kill your average trooper."

"I hear," said Davis, "that you can track as good as any Apache."

"Well, you heard right," said Sieber. "But there's only one of me and there's a thousand square miles of Apache country out there. That's what General Crook figured out. A thousand God-damn square miles.

"It takes an Apache to catch an Apache. White-eyes can't catch them alone. If it comes to a fight, most times we win. We got more guns. But we can't find them. That's the thing. The only way a band of Apache renegades is going to get found is by Apache scouts or pure damn fool luck. It's as simple as that."

In the middle of the next day, the nearly worn-out column of troops halted in the mountains to take a much-needed ten-minute break for rest, water, and smokes. Gatewood had Sergeant Mulrey station pickets in the rocks around them. Davis sat on a boulder with his carbine resting across his legs.

Standing nearby, Sieber watched as the Apache scouts strung themselves out across a high rock bluff. Ahead was the steepness of the Sierra Madres.

"You think the Apaches are somewhere close by, Mr. Sieber?" asked Davis.

"Hell," said Sieber, taking a bite from a plug of tobacco, "I don't think Geronimo's within a hundred miles of here."

Davis noticed a sudden intent expression on Sieber's face, and he followed the scout's look up into the rocks. There he saw Sergeant Turkey bounding over the rocks like a goat, stopping now and then to take another look. He tried to follow Sergeant Turkey's look, and then he saw in the distance a cloud of dust.

Davis took out his field glasses, first to watch the Apache scout and then to study the dust cloud on the horizon. For just an instant he saw men on horseback. Then they disappeared into a depression. He had not had time to identify them. The dust cloud was still visible though. He turned his attention back to Sergeant Turkey who was making his way quickly back to the main camp. Not far away, Gatewood was watching also. He looked at the approaching dust cloud through the battered field glasses he had exchanged with Geronimo.

Sieber ran the few steps across the rocks to stand by Gatewood's side. He watched the approaching dust cloud without the aid of glasses. It was drawing nearer, seeming to grow larger.

"Apaches don't make dust like that," said Gatewood.

"Lots of horses," said Sieber, squinting. "Maybe Federales. Maybe bandits. Same damn thing as far as I'm concerned."

Gatewood lowered his glasses and called out over his shoulder. "Sergeant Mulrey."

The sergeant ran up to Gatewood's side. "Sir," he said.

"Get horses detailed behind those rocks," said Gatewood, pointing. "Take cover in the formation there."

"Yes, sir," said Mulrey, running off to obey the command.

"Mr. Davis," Gatewood called.

Davis hurried over to join Gatewood and Sieber. All three men stared down and ahead, waiting for a chance to see who it was kicking up all that dust.

"Move over to the right flank," said Gatewood. "Keep order in the line. I don't want some damn fool firing a shot unless an order is given."

"Yes, sir," said Davis, and he trotted off to his new position just as Sergeant Turkey came running up to Sieber and Gatewood. Following his long run through the high rocks, the Apache was not even short of breath.

"Mexicanos," Turkey said.

"That's what I figured," said Sieber, shifting his chaw to the other side of his mouth. "How many?"

"Many Mexicanos," said Sergeant Turkey.

"¿Soldados o bandidos?" asked Gatewood.

"Don't make no difference," said Sieber. "Hell, they're all bandits down here. The whole damn country's nothing but thieves."

"Soldados," said Sergeant Turkey, ignoring

Sieber's comment. *"Hay mucho soldados. Mas or menos cuarenta."*

The troopers and scouts were all busy crawling over rocks, moving into position. Gatewood looked around and called out again.

"Sergeant Dutchy."

"There ain't nothing Apaches hate worse than Mexicans," said Sieber. "They even hate Mexicans worse than they hate us." He turned his face toward Sergeant Turkey. "Ain't that right, Sergeant?" he added.

The Apache scout remained silent, ignoring the question, and Dutchy came running forward. He stopped beside Gatewood.

"Sergeant Dutchy," said Gatewood, "take six scouts." He pointed to a rock ridge ahead and off to his right. "Move toward that point, along the ledge there."

"Real quick, Dutchy," said Sieber. "Pronto. On the double."

"Come with me," said Gatewood to Sieber and Sergeant Turkey, as Dutchy trotted off to obey the command. Gatewood led the way to a position on a rock bluff with a commanding view of the space beneath them. Down below behind a natural wall of rocks, they could see the Federales taking up a defensive position.

"Those bastards mess with us," said Sieber, "we'll send them packing."

"Mr. Sieber," said Gatewood, "I'm trying to prevent an international incident here, not provoke one."

He looked down toward the position to which he had sent Davis and called out. "Mr. Davis."

"Sir," answered Davis, looking up and around to locate Gatewood.

"Make our Mexican friends down there aware of our peaceful intentions," called Gatewood.

"Yes, sir."

Davis stood up to show himself to the Federales below. He waved an arm. No one among the Federales waved back.

"God-damned Mexicans," said Sieber. "What the hell are they up to?"

"Americanos," shouted Davis, again waving his arm. *"Americanos."*

Down below, a Federale took aim with a rifle and fired a shot. Another fired, and the bullets ricocheted off rocks near where Davis stood. Davis jumped back down and ducked behind the rocks for cover.

"Bastards," said Sieber. "What the damn hell are they doing?"

Davis, huddled for safety behind his boulder, yelled at the top of his voice.

"Damn it. *Americanos soldados. Americanos.*"

All was silent. There was no response from down below.

"Soldados Americanos," shouted Sieber. *"No fuego."*

Still the Federales were quiet. Gatewood called out over his shoulder. "Sergeant Mulrey."

"Here, sir."

"Move to the right flank," said Gatewood. "See

if you can get a good look at them. I want as accurate a count as possible of their number."

"Yes, sir," said Mulrey. He moved off and was soon out of Gatewood's sight. He climbed from one rock to another, trying to find a good position from which to look over and count the Federales below. Finding a chasm in front of him, he stood and jumped, landing safely on the next rock, but in so doing, he exposed himself for a moment to the Mexicans. A single shot rang out, and the bullet tore through Mulrey's midsection. He doubled over and collapsed.

Davis saw the whole thing, and he crawled out of his hole, scrambling to make his way to the wounded sergeant. A couple more shots were fired as he exposed himself briefly to the riflemen below, but he managed to reach the fallen Sergeant Mulrey without being hit. A few feet away from Mulrey, doubled up on his knees, Davis turned his head to call out in the direction of Gatewood.

"Mulrey's down," Davis shouted. "He's down."

He scurried on over to the sergeant's side, and, taking him by a shoulder, rolled him over onto his back. Then, looking into the staring eyes, he knew immediately that Mulrey was dead.

"Commence firing," Gatewood called out, and suddenly the air was shattered by the sound of the volleys from both sides. Gatewood fired off a couple of rounds, as did Sieber, but they were not in a good position to find many clear targets.

"First time I ever heard of the damn Mexican Army putting up a fight," said Sieber.

"The damn fools probably think that we're invading Mexico," said Gatewood. "Well, we're showing them some firepower."

"Damn right," said Sieber.

Rapid fire from both sides continued for another moment. Then Gatewood said to Sieber, "Now maybe they'll want to talk." He peered out carefully to look over his troops. "Troopers, cease fire!" he yelled. Then he called out to Davis, "Mr. Davis, see that all firing ceases in the ranks."

A shot rang out from below, striking the rocks near Gatewood. He huddled back down safely out of sight. All gunfire from the American troops had stopped. Gatewood tied a white handkerchief to the muzzle end of his Springfield. He looked around for a better position in the rocks, then ran for it. Sieber, keeping a little distance between them, followed. Bullets from the Federales chipped rocks along their path. Then Gatewood, finding his position, stood up boldly and waved the white flag.

"Soldados Americanos," he yelled. The firing from below ceased. There followed a tense moment of eerie, uneasy silence. The Mexican sun beat down unmercifully on the American soldiers scattered among the rocks. Then, at last, a voice came up from below.

"Usted. ¿Cuantos hombres en su compania?"

"We are American soldiers," shouted Gatewood, "pursuing hostile Apaches in accordance with an agreement between our two governments. Come out and talk."

He moved forward a little, and Sergeant Turkey stepped forward to stand at his right side.

"*¿Apaches?*" said the voice from below. "*¿Tiene Apaches?*"

Sieber moved forward to stand just to the left of Gatewood.

"Come on out here and talk, God damn it," he shouted.

Down below, a Mexican officer stood up from behind a rock.

"Come out and lay down your guns," he said. "You are in violation of Mexican sovereignty."

"We are looking for Geronimo," said Gatewood. "Geronimo. Our two countries have an agreement. Surely you know about it."

"Did you not hear me, *Señor?*" responded the Mexican. "I have not heard of any such agreement. Do as I say or face the consequences."

Sieber turned to Gatewood. "God damn Mexicans," he said. "You ain't going to give up our guns, are you?"

"Mr. Sieber," said Gatewood in a low voice, "an officer of the United States Army does not surrender his arms while facing a hostile force." He turned back toward the Mexicans below and raised his voice again. "We are members of the United States Army looking for Geronimo. We want to talk—"

A sudden volley of shots from below interrupted Gatewood, and to his right, he saw Sergeant Turkey grab his face with both hands. He looked as the Apache scout pitched forward, blood splattering from his face where it bashed onto the rocks.

Astonished, Gatewood quickly crouched behind the nearest rock. Sieber, vaulting to cover, was grazed alongside the head by a Mexican bullet. He screamed and fell, then dragged himself over behind a rock. Chato came from somewhere behind to scramble up to Sieber's side. Sieber held a hand to the side of his head, and blood ran freely between his fingers and down the side of his neck, soaking his buckskin shirt.

"Shit," he said. "They shot my damn ear. They shot my ear."

The shooting from below stopped, and the Mexican officer called out again.

"I demand that you surrender your arms," he said. "Do you understand? Surrender your arms. Then we will talk about this so-called agreement."

Chapter 13

To give proper emphasis to his ultimatum, the Federale officer, without warning, ordered another volley of shots. The American soldiers were all huddled down behind rocks for safety, awaiting further orders from their commander. Gatewood sat with his back against a boulder. Chato had moved over beside him. It was a hell of a fix he found himself in. The Federales did not seem to want to listen to reason, and Gatewood was not about to surrender to them. He had his orders, and, furthermore, he knew that they were in accordance with the international agreement between the United States and Mexico that allowed either army to cross the border if they were in actual pursuit of a band of "hostile Apaches." Gatewood did not want to fight the Mexicans and take a chance on starting a war with that country, but the Federale force below had left him little choice.

"Chato," he said, "it's time to win this fight. Move over there to the scouts on the flank. Tell them to fire at will."

As Chato moved out in a low crouch, Gatewood turned his head in the opposite direction and called out to the troopers there.

"Resume firing," he said, and again the air was alive with bullets.

Chato scrambled over the rock formation with bullets smacking around him. As he moved, he signaled the Apache scouts to fire back from the high rocks. He continued to move farther along the right flank until he reached the second group of scouts who had been stationed there with Dutchy. Then, with Dutchy and Chato leading them, the scouts soon flanked the Federales.

Oblivious to the movement of the Apache scouts, the Federales continued sending a withering fusillade in the direction of the American troops. Then, from his new position, Dutchy raised his rifle, took careful aim and fired. Down below, a Federale screamed and fell back. The other Apache scouts began firing, and the Mexicans suddenly found themselves caught in a deadly crossfire. Moving back toward their horses in a sudden panic, they left seven dead Federales behind them at their previous line of defense.

They clambered onto their horses and then hastily retreated even farther away from the rocks out onto the flat of the desert and safely beyond rifle range. There they seemed to mill around for a moment of confusion before they actually began their full-scale withdrawal.

From his rock-perch vantage point, Gatewood stood and watched the dust of the inglorious retreat curl away across the plain. Sieber, still clutching the side of his head, blood still oozing, walked over to stand beside him.

"Run, you sons of bitches!" he called out at the top of his lungs. "Run, God damn you!" Then he lowered his voice. "Shoot a man's God-damn ear off," he said. "Hell."

Gatewood turned in time to see Dutchy walking up from behind. He was carrying Sergeant Turkey in his arms like a child. Tears were streaming down the dark cheeks of the scout, carving furrows in the caked layer of alkali dust that covered his face. He knelt to lay the body out delicately on the hard rocks.

Gatewood moved over to kneel beside him. He looked at Sergeant Turkey, whose shattered head was wrapped in Dutchy's dirty shirt, now soaked through with blood.

"Sergeant," he said, "can you hear me?"

Sergeant Turkey's eyes rolled toward Gatewood, but he made no response. Gatewood could see that the bullet had gone through the scout's brain. He knew that the wound was mortal.

"He can't hear nothing," said Sieber. "Shit. This damn ear hurts. I never have no kind of luck."

Sergeant Turkey continued to stare blankly at Gatewood.

"Sergeant?" said Gatewood, still trying to communicate with the dying man.

"He is my cousin," said Dutchy, the tears still running freely down his face. "He is my family."

Sieber gave Dutchy a curious look of genuine surprise.

"Well, I'll be damned," Sieber said. "First time for everything. I thought they never cried. I sure never seen it before."

"Be quiet, Mr. Sieber," said Gatewood. He stood up and walked over to Davis who was standing nearby. "Tell me about Sergeant Mulrey," he said.

"It was a clean wound," said Davis. "I think it killed him instantly."

Gatewood took several deep breaths. He stood looking off into the distance, not toward anyone. Davis thought then that Gatewood did not have as hard an edge to him as he tried to show the world.

"We'll head back for the border in the morning," Gatewood said.

Sieber quickly stepped up close and looked Gatewood in the face. He looked as if he could not quite believe what he had just heard. He certainly did not want to believe it.

"Crook ain't going to like it," he said. "Us coming back empty-handed."

"None of us like it, Mr. Sieber," said Gatewood, "but we don't have enough provisions to stick it out any longer. We're low on food, low on ammunition, and we've lost some important personnel. Besides, the men are worn out. If it came to a fight with Geronimo, they wouldn't be worth a damn."

Sieber turned away disgusted. He spat a stream of brown liquid which splattered on a flat rock. Then he pulled a bandanna out of his hip pocket which he held up to his torn and bloody ear. Gatewood ignored him and turned to Davis.

"Mr. Davis, we travel at dawn," Gatewood said.

"Yes, sir," said Davis.

Gatewood then moved off by himself, with Davis and Sieber watching after him.

"Damn," said Sieber. "There ain't nothing that bleeds like a damn tore ear."

The following morning, a half a mile from the company bivouac, the entire command was assembled in formation near two fresh graves. Many of the battle-hardened faces were streaked with tears. At the grave site, Sieber and two troopers had sung a hymn. Gatewood held a Bible in his hands. He spoke out loudly to the entire assembly.

"These men," he said, "found a shallow grave in a foreign land. There won't be any flowers. Their families will never find this place to visit—to pay their respects. The only laurels they can ever have are those that you men might win for them. We're here at the ragged end of everything. Very few care about the cavalry. So we have to care about each other."

Gatewood paused to look over the faces of his men, and to try to regain control of his voice, which had come dangerously near to choking up on him. Then he went on.

"We know their bravery: Thomas Mulrey, formerly of the Army of Virginia, Sergean the White Mountain Apaches. These me the esteem of their comrades in arms."

He paused again and looked down at the fresh graves which held the bodies of men he had spoken with only the day before, men who had been alive and well and young enough to have had years of life left before them.

"I could read any number of passages from the Bible that might be deemed appropriate," he said, "but—" Again he paused, almost losing control of his voice. He swallowed hard and took a deep breath. "But I want to say . . . the first prayer that I learned . . . from my mother.

"Gentle Jesus, meek and mild, look upon this little child. Pity his simplicity. Suffer him to come to thee. Amen."

He turned abruptly and walked away without another word. Davis knew that Gatewood was done. He gave a nod to the Apache scouts who then raised their rifles to their shoulders and fired a salute into the air. Gatewood turned and walked back over to stop beside Davis.

"Post double pickets a half mile in each direction," he said. "You take the first duty. Dismiss the assembly."

"Yes, sir," said Davis. "You get to bury quite a few men in the cavalry. Don't you, sir?"

"Mr. Davis," said Gatewood, "men have been killing each other since Adam's sons. To die for an idea can be noble, but it would be a lot more noble if men died for ideas that were true."

As Gatewood slowly walked away, obviously deeply affected by the deaths of Sergeant Mulrey and Sergeant Turkey, Sieber and the two troopers beside the graves began another hymn. Their voices carried off toward the horizon, as Lieutenant Davis moved to carry out his most recent orders.

Chapter 14

General Crook sat behind his desk at the far end of the squad room in the military headquarters at San Carlos. The back and seat of the heavy wooden chair were covered with leather, and every time the general moved, the leather creaked. Al Sieber sat in a straight chair across the desk from the general. Crook was reading aloud from a document he held in his hands.

> Thereby, I tender my resignation as Commander of this Department. I have served you well in the past, but my judgment has been called into question. It shames me to do this after so long and frustrating a struggle. I have obviously made a grievous error in trusting the word of Geronimo that he would surrender.

Sieber silently agreed with Crook on that issue, and, he thought, had the general asked his opinion in the first place he would have told him not to trust the old bastard. But then, he knew that Crook would not have listened to him anyhow. He was a good man, Sieber thought, but like most, too trusting for his own good.

Perhaps others will be more correct or more fortunate. The real tragedy, I know you do not understand, is to the Apache people. They have lost in me a true friend, and they have few.

George Crook,
Brigadier General,
United States Army.

Crook folded the document and set it aside. He looked up at Sieber, and Sieber noted that the general's face seemed more worn, more haggard and drawn than before. The long campaign against the Apaches and its attendant frustrations seemed to have aged him more than time alone could have done.

"I was forced to send this to Washington a few days ago," Crook said. "They have accepted my resignation with regrets. General Nelson Miles will replace me." He paused and stared at the desk top in front of him.

"Nothing to be done, General?" asked Sieber.

"Nothing," said Crook. "A graceful resignation for the general who couldn't catch Geronimo."

The general stood up abruptly and walked to the

window in the front wall of the room, looking out onto the dark parade ground outside. "Miles," he said. "Nelson Miles. They'll replace me with Miles. That damn storekeeper."

Sieber cleared his throat nervously.

"Al?" said Crook, turning to look at the scout. "You ever think about why we're out here? What the hell we're doing? I mean the whole thing. The Indians were here. We arrive, push them out, hunt them down if they fight back."

"Hell, General," said Sieber, "that's the whole history of the country. Far as the Apache goes, they took the land from the Navajo and the Comanche. And before that, the Navajos and Comanches took it from the scorpions and rattlesnakes and any other belly crawling creature that God threw down here. Ain't right or wrong. It's the way it is."

"Settlers, prospectors, land speculators," said Crook, "they don't admit it, but the truth is they all want the Indians dead. They see the army as their weapon. But the army that fights the Apaches is really the best hope of keeping them alive. Only the army can protect them."

"I fought them a long time," said Sieber. "I figure if I was an Apache, I'd be standing right next to Geronimo shooting at the blue coats. But God made me who I am. Between them or us, I figure it's us."

"Yeah, but damn it, Al, is this the only way we could win?"

"I don't have the answer to that one, General," said Sieber. "I'm only a hired hand."

"The Apaches are in for a hard road, Al," said

Crook. "The future's against them if they don't change. Then would they still be Apaches? I don't have the answers either."

Sieber stood up and extended his hand. Crook took it in his for a firm handshake. "Just wanted to say it, General," said Sieber. "I didn't always agree with you, but you always had my respect. While you was in charge, the army was a proper piece of work." He picked his hat up off the desk and put it on his head. "I'm quitting this damn fool job," he said. "I'm going to go down to Tombstone and get drunk."

"Take care, Al," said Crook.

"Yessir," said the scout, and he turned and walked out of the office for the last time.

Brigadier General Nelson A. Miles, hungry for promotion, eagerly replaced Crook when given the chance. He had fought the Comanches in Texas. He had chased Crazy Horse and Sitting Bull in the Yellowstone country, where he had been given the name Bear Coat by the Sioux. He had taken part in the relentless pursuit of Chief Joseph and the Nez Perce, who had been trying to reach the safety of Canada. And where Crook had failed, he knew that he would succeed. He would capture Geronimo.

He waited in his new quarters until he knew that the troops would be properly assembled out on the parade ground. He was properly attired in his military uniform, sharp, but not formal. He checked himself one last time in the full-length mirror on the wall, then walked to the door and opened it. He stepped outside onto the porch.

A combat column of two hundred men stood to horse, ready to move out. He looked them over from his vantage point on the porch, and they met with his approval. They had been well prepared for him, he thought.

In front of the porch an orderly stood at attention holding Miles's horse. Miles stepped down off the porch and took the reins from the orderly. He mounted the charger smartly.

"General Miles, sir," the officer of the day called out, snapping off a salute. Miles returned the salute just as smartly. "Sixth Cavalry detail for maneuvers, ready, sir."

Miles rode to the front and center of the assembly. He sat in the saddle with military stiffness, and he spoke in a loud, clear voice. He was in his late forties, but he was still strong and robust. His steely eyes were clear. His full mustache was waxed and turned up slightly at the ends.

The soldiers watching him could tell already that his command would be very different from that of Crook. The contrast between the two brigadier generals could not have been sharper.

"I'm honored to be here with you men of the Sixth Cavalry," said Miles, "honored to be here by order of the President of the United States.

"We are charged with bringing in the renegade Apache Geronimo. We will accomplish our task. We will succeed. But we are abandoning certain practices of the past, such as overreliance on Apache scouts, men of divided loyalties.

"I will keep troops in the field until the enemy is fully subjugated, fully pacified. There will be no compromise with the honor of our nation. There will be no compromise with the honor of the United States Army."

Miles wrapped up his introductory speech to the Sixth Cavalry with a sharp salute, and the regimental military band began to play a rousing march.

"Lieutenant," called Miles.

"Sir," responded the lieutenant, then gave a nod to the first sergeant.

The first sergeant turned to the troops. "Prepare to mount," he called out. He paused long enough for the troops to do so, then added, "Mount."

The band continued to play as the troopers swung into their saddles. Then the lieutenant took up the commands to start the column moving.

General Miles kept his position and watched the troops ride away, out of the compound, on their first patrol under his command. The usual crowd of soldiers left behind, soldiers' wives, and a variety of civilians including Apaches and Mexicans stood by watching as well. Gatewood and Davis had been left out of this detail, and they stood side by side and saluted as the column passed them by.

Inside the squad room, Gatewood sat at a desk filling out some forms. An orderly stepped into the room, stood at attention, and called out, "General Miles, sir." Gatewood and the others in the room stood for Miles's entrance and saluted. Miles walked through the room heading toward his own office. He returned the salute and was about to go through the door. Gatewood and the others had resumed their seats.

Miles paused and looked back over his shoulder. "Gatewood," he said.

Gatewood stood again. "Sir," he said.

"I doubt you enjoy your new assignment," said Miles. "There's nothing personal about it, son. I hear that you're a fine officer."

"Thank you, sir," said Gatewood.

"I was sent here to use a new broom," said the general. "I'm afraid you were too closely identified with the previous command."

"Sir," said Gatewood, "I was proud to serve with General Crook."

"Yes, indeed," said Miles. "I expect you were. He's a fine man. But a failed policy is a failed policy. As you were, Lieutenant."

Miles moved on into his office followed by an aide who shut the door behind them. Gatewood continued standing and stared at the door. He knew the army well, knew that commands changed and his job was simply to follow orders. Yet he could not shake the feeling of loss that weighed down on his soul.

It had something to do with his heartfelt belief that General Crook, for all his faults, was a much better man for the job than was Miles. Crook had not always understood the Apaches, but he did have a certain amount of compassion. Gatewood did not know Miles, but he knew the general's reputation. He knew that, in spite of his public comments which were always tactful, Crook had nothing but scorn for Miles, a merchant who, at the beginning of the Civil War, had purchased a commission for himself. And Miles had a certain coldblooded reputation as well. Crook had been right about one thing: The future of Geronimo and the Apaches did not look good.

Twenty Mexican Federales, tired and ragged from a long desert patrol, crossed a shallow creek in the Sonoran desert. Some rode, some walked and led their horses. Two mules carried the bodies of dead Apaches slung over their backs. Three young Apache women, their hands bound behind their backs, were being shoved along rudely. There was a bounty on the heads of Apache males in Mexico. The women would be sold into slavery. It was obvious from the sad looks of these Federales that they had gone through a hard fight for their prizes.

The officer in charge called a halt for a rest. A guard stood wearily over the Apache women. The tired and beaten men dropped to the ground where they stood. A few made their way over to the stream to drop their heads into the water, to drink, or simply to cool themselves off. The officer stood alert, looking around at the dry hills beyond. He heard a shout and then a dull thwack.

He looked around and saw the guard he had left with the women, still on his feet with an arrow through his neck. Horror-stricken and desperate, the man reached for the arrow with both hands. His throat made involuntary gurgling, gagging sounds. His eyes slowly glazed over, and he fell forward dead.

"Apaches!" someone yelled.

The tired men, rejuvenated by fear, ran for their horses and grabbed for their weapons.

"Geronimo!" someone shouted.

"Apache."

The Apaches seemed to come from all around, from behind rocks, from inside tangles of dry brush, out of the very ground. Some were armed with rifles, some with bows and arrows. Some fired their weapons from a distance, while others rushed in on the unprepared Federales with knives flashing. One Apache crushed the skull of a Federale with a stone-headed war club.

The officer managed to get on his horse. He drew his revolver and turned to aim at an Apache, but his horse was shot from under him. He managed to jump free and scramble to his feet. He aimed again, but before he could fire, a rifle bullet tore through his chest.

Suddenly it was over, as quickly as it had begun. Most of the Federales were dead. A few wounded were still alive, whimpering and moaning, and the Apache warriors sought them out to dispatch them. Then Geronimo appeared, a .45 revolver in his hand. He walked over to stand beside a wounded Federale. The man looked up and began to beg for mercy. Calmly, Geronimo pointed his revolver at the man's head and fired.

He holstered the revolver and pulled out a big bowie knife, then walked over to the women and cut their bindings. The few wounded who had not yet been killed still cried for mercy.

"Geronimo," one cried out. He was on his knees, reaching toward Geronimo, pleading for mercy. A warrior stepped up behind him, grabbed him by the hair and pulled his head back. Then with a knife in his other hand, he slit the man's throat.

"Gokhlaye," said one of the freed women, calling Geronimo by his Apache name. "Gokhlaye."

Chapter 15

Back in Arizona Territory, Mangas lay atop a huge boulder, high in the rocks, overlooking the wide expanse of desert below. His rifle was laid across the top of the boulder. A short distance behind him, Geronimo, Ulzana, and other Apaches sat on their horses and watched. Mangas's horse stood with them waiting.

Below, pulled by six mules, a covered wagon lumbered its slow way across the hot desert sands. Mangas sighted in carefully on the driver, and squeezed the trigger. The rifle bucked, and its loud report echoed across the desert, ripping into the still, heavy, silent air. Down below, the unsuspecting driver jerked, then slumped forward to topple from the wagon box. It was a good shot.

Geronimo barked out a command and turned his

horse. The others followed him as Mangas ran to jump on the back of his own waiting mount. The Apaches raced down from the hills toward the wagon and mules, anxious to see what supplies they would find there.

A young lieutenant, ordered out by Miles with a column of twenty troopers, rode across the open desert in Sonora, Mexico. Eight pack mules brought up the rear. There was nothing in sight but a vast stretch of rolling dunes. Then, unexpectedly, the wind began to blow, raising a sudden, blinding sandstorm.

The lieutenant called a halt. Troopers coughed and covered their eyes. Some wrapped bandannas around their faces for protection against the biting sand. The storm was so fierce, and the blowing sand was so thick, that they could barely see each other and could not recognize the man standing next to them. It was all they could do to control their panicking horses.

And then figures like ghosts seemed to rise up on all sides right out of the desert floor. They were Apaches, and they had done just that. Lying down and covering themselves with sand, they had waited for the arrival of the column. Each held a repeating rifle and carried a revolver, and as they rose up from the soft ground, they began to fire at the shadows of the soldiers in the blowing sand.

The soldiers were caught in a deadly crossfire, totally unprepared, completely involved in protecting themselves from the storm and in trying to manage the horses. As they realized what was happening, they had to turn loose the animals to reach for their weapons. Few of them ever got off a shot.

The sounds of the shots from the Apache rifles and the sounds of screaming men and horses ripped the howling of the wind. As they fired, the Apaches moved in closer, tightening the deadly circle. Some stopped shooting and drew their knives. The troopers, caught first by the blinding sandstorm, then completely surprised by the Apaches, were totally overwhelmed in a matter of minutes. They were hardly even able to offer a feeble defense.

When the shooting was over, twenty troopers and a young lieutenant lay dead upon the blood-soaked desert ground. The wind continued to sweep the scene with stinging, blowing sand. The Apache figures moving about to catch up horses and gather newly acquired weapons and ammunition were still silhouettes in the storm. One of them was Geronimo.

The sun had begun to show itself, bringing a little warmth to the cluster of wickieups in the copse beside the river. It had been a cold night in the high country in Mexico. The camp was flanked on both sides by brush and boulders. High hills rose behind.

At one end of the camp a small herd of horses grazed, as women began building up fires to start the day. Two men walked together toward the edge of camp away from the horse herd.

Shots rang out, and the two men jerked and yelled and fell, each riddled by several bullets. The whole camp came suddenly to life. Women ran screaming for their children, and men hurried to get their weapons and searched the surrounding area to locate their attackers.

Geronimo came out of a wickieup, a rifle in one hand, his revolver belt in the other. He looked around quickly and saw that the camp was being attacked from three sides. There was only one direction to go. Around him, men, women, and children were falling, struck down by bullets.

"Look out for the horses," he yelled, but then the bullets seemed to come faster from all three sides. One young man, trying to get to the herd, was dropped by a rifle shot.

"Let the horses go," he cried. "Soldiers and Apache scouts are on both sides and above us. Let the women and children run to the river. Men, stay behind."

Women and children and a few men ran for the river, many of them falling before they reached it. For a while, the warriors tried to stay behind them to defend their escape, but the barrage was too heavy. They turned and ran for the river. Then a fourth group of Apache scouts rose up from near the river and began to shoot.

"Don't shoot the women and children," someone shouted, but the plea seemed to have little effect. Some of the people, seeing no place to run to, stopped and held up their hands in surrender. Some were shot down with their hands in the air.

"Scatter and go as you can," cried Geronimo. Dodging bullets, he ran for the brush and made his way somehow between the soldiers and scouts who were hidden there. He ran until he knew he was safe, safe for the time being. How many, he wondered, were killed? How many captured? How many, like himself, had escaped the surprise attack?

Geronimo led his small band of twenty-four warriors across the open desert. They walked their mounts, leading extra horses and mules. It was a still day, and the sun burned down over all. Mangas rode beside Geronimo.

All of the Apaches showed tired, drawn faces. Some of them had been wounded. All of them were weary and battle scarred. From somewhere behind, Geronimo heard one say, speaking in Apache, "The White-eyes are crazy. We kill many. Still they come. Why don't they leave us alone?"

"There's no rest," said another. "White-eyes on one side of the line and Mexicans on the other."

Geronimo understood how the young men felt. The same questions about the White-eyes were in his own mind, and he did not know the answers. They were like no one else. They wanted everything for themselves, and they wanted the Apaches to live like white men. At least that was what they said they wanted. But when the Apaches quit fighting and moved to the reservation, the White-eye soldiers told them they had to stay put. White men did not live like prisoners in their own land. Really, Geronimo thought, they wanted the Apaches all dead.

And the Mexicans—well, Geronimo did not want peace with the Mexicans. He could not imagine a life in which he did not kill Mexicans whenever he got a chance. He remembered finding the bodies of his young wife and their two daughters, killed at the hands of Mexicans. He would die fighting, before he would ever make peace with them.

Farther back in line, a young man, weak from his wounds, slipped from the back of his horse to land on the hard ground with a dull thud and a loud groan. They all stopped at once, and another young man jumped off his horse to run to the side of the fallen one.

Geronimo turned his horse and rode back close to the scene. He looked down at the young man lying there, and he could see that the hurt warrior did not have long to live. He had been badly wounded, and he had born up bravely, but he would not last much longer. Geronimo felt sad for this young man, but he felt proud of him at the same time.

Mangas rode to Geronimo's side and looked down at the fallen man. "Can he stay on his horse until we get back to camp?" asked Mangas.

"It's too late," said the young man who knelt beside his wounded companion. Then the fallen one struggled, trying desperately to get to his feet. He did not want to slow the march. He did not want to be left behind. He would ride if he could. He managed to get up on one elbow, but the strain was too much. He slumped back. He was dead.

"We can't go on like this," said Mangas. "Attacking. Running. Hiding. We'll all die."

"You speak like a coward," accused Ulzana.

"I want to be with my family," said a young man. "The reservation was a bad place, but it was better than this."

Geronimo knew their feelings. He even shared them, but he could not let them know that. He also knew how treacherous the white men could be.

"Do you want to go to a fort and surrender?" Geronimo asked. "Do you want to see how long you will live there? Do you think they'll tell us that we will be forgiven? This way, if we die, we die free."

Back at San Carlos, Gatewood received word that General Miles wanted to see him. It was an unusual request. Since his arrival at his new post, Miles had practically ignored Gatewood. He had given him the courtesy once of telling him why. Gatewood was too closely associated with Crook for the storekeeper's taste. Now it could only be one thing, Gatewood thought. He's not making progress against Geronimo fast enough.

He walked directly across the empty parade ground in the dark of the night wondering also why Miles had chosen this unusual hour for his interview. He walked into the squad room as he had been told. It was dark, and it seemed empty. Then in a far corner, a match was struck. General Miles lit a lamp, and in the eerie light, Gatewood saw the general looking at him.

"Lieutenant," said Miles, "I doubt you're enjoying your current assignment. Nothing personal. I hear you're a fine officer. Do you know why I've brought you here, Mr. Gatewood?"

"No, sir," said Gatewood, "but I expect it's got something to do with Geronimo."

"Tomorrow," said Miles, "a policy change will be announced. As punishment for Geronimo's resistance, all Chiricahua currently living on reservation land are to be rounded up and sent to Florida. They will be kept there at the very least until Geronimo is captured or killed. That is a harsh penalty that he's brought down on his own people."

Miles studied Gatewood's face as if looking for some response, but he saw none. "People tell me you two are friendly," he said.

Gatewood couldn't quite tell how the general meant that statement. He thought that he had detected a slight accusatory tone. He was wary, and he answered cautiously. "Sir," he said, "any relationship I may have had with Geronimo has not in any way compromised my effectiveness in the field."

"At ease, Lieutenant," said Miles. "You're an officer in the United States Army, and I would not do you the indignity of questioning your loyalty. But I need you to speak freely with me. Are you friendly with Geronimo? Can you find him and talk to him?"

Gatewood took a deep breath and contemplated the general's question for a moment. "I thought so once," he said. "Now, I've got no way to be sure."

"Why not?" asked Miles.

Gatewood thought that there had been so many lies told and there had been so much unnecessary killing that no sane Apache would believe anything

any white man ever said again. How could any
Apache claim anything like friendship with any
white man? But he knew that he couldn't say these
things to General Miles.

"He's tired and hungry," Gatewood said instead.
"Maybe he's even a little scared. That's a dangerous
combination in any man, sir."

"The signs indicate that he's starving, or pretty
close to it," said Miles. "Living on rabbits and
cactus. I know, because now I've got five thousand
troops stretching from here to Chihuahua searching for—"

"Only thirty-five Apaches, sir," said Gatewood.
"Or less. That's what I think he'll be down to in a
month."

"Thirty-five starving Apaches," said Miles.

Gatewood was well aware that Miles had five
thousand soldiers in the field, and he knew that
figure represented one-third of the combat strength
of the entire United States Army. The general also
had five hundred Apache scouts, and there were
thousands of irregular civilian militia roaming the
deserts and the mountains in search of Geronimo.
In addition to all of that, Gatewood knew that
Geronimo was constantly being pursued by thousands of Mexican troops. All of that for thirty or so
bedraggled Apache warriors.

Gatewood found it all supremely ironic that
Geronimo and his small band of battered warriors
had become a major problem for the United States
Army in all its might. What was he costing them,
these men who looked down their noses on him as

something not quite human? How much money was he costing the government? How many lives was he costing the military? How many careers?

"Begging the general's pardon," he said, "but why not leave Geronimo to the Mexicans? He can't continue raiding across the border. He can't afford to lose any more warriors, and he's got no way to replace them."

"That's not good enough," said Miles. "The political situation demands results."

It occurred to Gatewood that it might have been the ambition of General Miles that demanded results, but, of course, he kept that thought to himself, too.

"You're going to help me bring that murdering bastard to justice," the general continued, "because you're his one chance in hell of getting out of this thing alive. You've got to find him, Gatewood. Here. Make him this proposal."

Miles handed Gatewood a piece of paper. Gatewood took it, unfolded it, and began to read.

"I have the authority," said Miles, not waiting for Gatewood to finish reading the paper, "to hunt down the son of a bitch all the way to South America if I have to, but I want this nonsense to come to an end. I can give you all the scouts you need, a forty-man detail, regular cavalry plus a mule pack train."

"I'd never get close to Geronimo with even ten men, sir," said Gatewood, looking up from the paper.

"How many do you want, Lieutenant?"

"Three," said Gatewood, "and I'd like to pick them myself."

"I suppose Lieutenant Davis is one," said the general.

"I had him in mind, sir. And Al Sieber. Him and Chato. I need them to scout."

"Sieber quit his job," said Miles abruptly. "And besides, I was given to understand that you and he don't get along well."

"I can get him back," said Gatewood, ignoring the second part of Miles's response. "There's nothing he likes better than hunting Geronimo. He's a good tracker, and he's good in a fight, if it comes to that."

"Whatever happens, Lieutenant," said Miles, "this conversation never took place. Any negotiations with Geronimo must be strictly confidential. Is that understood?"

"Two years in Florida?" Gatewood asked, referring to the paper.

"Two years in Florida," said Miles. "With their families. When they return to the reservation here in Arizona Territory, each warrior gets forty acres of land and two mules."

Gatewood paused, uneasy. When he spoke again, it was carefully, almost tentative. Militarily, he was about to step on shaky ground, and he knew it well.

"Sir," he said, "there's just one thing . . ."

"What's that, Lieutenant?"

"I don't believe that you or the government intend to keep this promise."

"I'm ordering you to offer it," said Miles. "None of the rest is your concern."

Gatewood stood silent while the general gave him an icy stare. He knew that the casual conversation had come to an end.

"Lieutenant," said Miles, "you have your orders."

For a moment Gatewood returned the general's stare. He'd been handed the devil's bargain, he figured, but, then, he was a soldier. He snapped to attention and saluted.

"Sir," he said.

Gatewood stood that evening at the opening in the front of his tent looking out over the parade ground. He felt a profound sadness. He knew that he could easily lose his life on the mad mission that General Miles had given him, but a soldier always faced that risk. What bothered him, what gave him this sense that he might be facing the crack of doom, was the heartfelt belief that Miles and the United States government were wrong and that he might well die for a cause in which he did not believe.

The last orange rays of light were falling across San Carlos, and a military band was playing a light air across the way. He turned away from the tent opening and moved over to a small desk. He pulled out the chair and sat behind the desk, taking up a pen to write by the light of an oil-burning lamp.

"My dear Georgia," he wrote.

Tomorrow I begin an expedition into Mexico that I feel sure will bring me once again face to face with Geronimo. I don't want you to feel unnecessary stress, but honesty forces me to say that this may be the last time I am able to write to you. Where I am going, the risks will be very high.

I have volunteered for this duty because it is expected of me, but in truth I despise myself for doing so. In my heart I wish nothing more than to return home to Virginia and be with my family.

As you know, Dear, you are the one person in my life I have ever been able to confide in—confide things that I can tell no one else.

I leave at dawn tomorrow, and I am afraid—deeply afraid that I will never see you or our children again.

He signed the letter and folded it carefully, then leaned back in his chair. He thought about General Miles and his arrogance and pomposity. He thought about Crook and his sometimes misguided, paternalistic compassion for the Apaches. He thought about Al Sieber, whom he had never liked, and whom he was now prepared to enlist again for this new and dangerous mission. And he realized that for all of the old scout's rough ways and seeming cold-heartedness, he would much prefer his plain and honest company to that of either Miles or Crook. He thought of Geronimo and the rest of the Apaches, and he wondered what treachery and what miseries were in store for them. But, most of all, he thought of his home in Virginia and the wife and children waiting for him there.

Chapter 16

And so First Lieutenant Charles B. Gatewood, with his small handpicked party, rode once more across the border into the Mexican desert. The two army lieutenants had not discussed their feelings regarding their mission, but Davis was still silently longing for the world of just and righteous action that had led him to become a soldier. The grinding glare of the hot sun overhead seemed to him to have driven that and every other noble human quality out of the world.

He wasn't sure about Gatewood. At times he thought that Gatewood felt as he did, that the United States Army was not upholding justice on the frontier. Yet there had been other times when Gatewood had seemed to Davis to be little more than a polished version of Sieber.

Specific knowledge regarding Gatewood's attitude and feelings was, of course, of no practical use or real need to Davis. Gatewood was his superior officer, and Davis was a soldier. He had planned and prepared for a military career, and he would carry out the orders he was given whether or not he agreed with or understood them. Still, Gatewood puzzled him.

One hundred fifty miles into the Sierra Madres, they spotted black smoke ahead. They were not afraid of riding into an ambush, for Sieber and Chato had been scouting in advance for some miles. They had likely already come upon the source of the smoke. So Gatewood and Davis kicked up their mounts to hurry ahead and join them.

They soon found the two scouts at the sorry sight of a burning village. Wickieups still smoldered, and bodies were strewn about the clearing. A dead man was tied upright to a post. He had been scalped. Chato was kneeling over the body of a dead woman. The whole place had been devastated.

Gatewood rode on into the ruined village, looking around at the carnage. Davis, horrified, dismounted at the edge of the ruin and stared into it with stunned disbelief. Gatewood pulled his horse to a halt near where Chato still knelt, there by the body.

"Who are they?" Gatewood asked.

"They are Yaquis," said Chato. "Not Apaches."

He straightened himself up to stand there beside the lieutenant's horse.

"Yaquis?" asked Gatewood. "Why would anyone do this to Yaquis?"

"White men came at dawn," said Chato. "They attacked when these Yaquis were sleeping." He pointed east. "They came out of the rising sun."

Sieber just then came backing out of a smoldering but still intact wickieup. He looked around and found a stool, bent and picked it up. The body of a Yaqui man was lying not far from where the stool had been and only a few strides away from where Chato had knelt by the woman's body. Sieber glanced at the two bodies, put the stool upright on the ground and sat. A scrawny dog ran by with its tail tucked tightly between its legs.

Davis came walking up at last, slowly, still staring with disbelief at the bodies lying around in grotesque positions. He was leading his own mount and the mules. He stopped near Sieber and looked at him, astounded to see the man sitting so casually between two dead and mutilated bodies. Sieber gestured toward the wickieup behind him.

"There's two more dead in there," he said. "Two little kids. They scalped them all—all four of them. Mama and daddy and kids. Whole damn family."

Davis was unable to hide the bewilderment and horror he was feeling. Sieber looked at him and read the expression.

"Bounty hunters," he explained. "The Mexican government pays two hundred pesos a head for the men. One hundred for the women. Fifty for those kids."

"Jesus," said Davis.

"Sons of bitches," said Sieber. "They'll kill any Indian, then claim it's an Apache. The government can't tell a Yaqui scalp from an Apache scalp, so they pay." He looked off toward the distant horizon. "I don't see how any fellow can sink that low," he said. "Must be Texans. Lowest form of white man there is."

"Most of the men got away," said Chato, pointing away from the village. "They're up in the hills. They'll come back in one day, maybe two. They'll come back for their families."

Davis stood silent, listening to the explanations and still staring at the devastation. He wanted to look away, but, somehow, he could not. He found himself horribly fascinated.

"They'll build big fire," Chato continued. "Burn the bodies. Then go join with other Yaqui tribe. Maybe find new wives. Make new babies."

Gatewood swung down out of his saddle and stepped over to Chato. His face was grim and determined.

"You and Sieber," he said. "I want you to track those bounty hunters."

"They go off that way," said Chato. "To the hills. After they hunt Yaqui men, they head for Soyopas to get their money."

Gatewood stepped in closer to Chato and looked him in the face. "I promise you, Chato," he said, "we're going to catch the men that did this thing— this—terrible thing. This act of—barbarism. I promise you." Then he switched to the Apache language and added, "From my heart."

Chato shrugged. He would track who they told him to track, but he did have a hard time understanding why a bluecoat who had killed Apaches seemed to be so stricken by the dead Yaquis. As far as Chato could tell, the scalp hunters had as much reason to kill the Yaquis as the bluecoats had to kill Apaches. It didn't worry him, though. He had long since stopped trying to figure out the White-eyes.

Gatewood next turned his attention to Sieber, who was still sitting on the stool. "And I don't give a damn what you say about it, Al," he said. "I don't want to hear about what the general would say when he finds out I've taken valuable time away from our mission. I don't—"

"Lieutenant," said Sieber, "you ain't going to hear no complaints from me, and the general ain't going to hear nothing about this little side trip either. Not as far as I'm concerned. There's only one thing though."

"What's that, Al?" asked Gatewood.

"You better not be too far behind me," said Sieber, "'cause, if you are, them bastards are likely to all be dead by the time you catch up."

On a rock plateau high in the Mexican mountains, Geronimo walked quietly through his Sierra Madre campground of ten wickieups, looking past what was left of his ragtag band. It was late evening, and it was cold in the mountains. He moved under a tattered ramada to squat beside a young Chiricahua man, shivering under a threadbare blanket. The young man's feet protruded from under the blanket, and Geronimo could see that the moccasins had holes in the soles with bloodstains around them.

The young man noticed Geronimo and started to sit up, the look on his face anxious, eager.

"You need me?" he asked. "I'm ready."

"You're sick," said Geronimo. "I need you to be healthy. Rest. The women have gathered some medicine for you."

"Do we leave at dawn?" asked the young man, his voice weak.

"No," said Geronimo. "We're safe here for a while. We'll wait, but not for long. Go to sleep now."

The young man closed his eyes and lay back to relax. Geronimo stood up and walked to the edge of the plateau. He turned his face to the sky and closed his eyes. A medicine bag was clasped between his hands.

His people were worn out. They were hungry and sick, and many of them were wounded. Many were dying. They wanted to go home, yet Geronimo knew in his heart that they could not go home. Some were urging him to surrender, but they did not know what would happen if he did that. They thought they would be taken back to the reservation as before. Geronimo knew that it was too late for that. He knew that if he surrendered, at the very least, they would all be made prisoners. How could he tell them? How could he make them understand? He did not know what to do. He stayed there on the edge of the plateau with his eyes closed, and he felt the wind begin to blow.

"I have just seen my power," he said, as if

speaking to something unseen. "A White-eye will be coming soon. I have seen a vision. A White-eye will be coming soon."

They rode grimly toward the mountains, following the lead of Chato. They forgot that they were tired and dirty and hungry. Davis, for the first time since his arrival in Arizona Territory, felt a strong sense of purpose. He was on a mission, the purpose of which he felt deeply, and, also for the first time, he felt that all of his companions, for all their differences, shared that sense of purpose.

They were not following orders or army policy. They wore civilian clothes, and they had, in a very real sense, ceased to be soldiers or even employees of the army. They were four men who had shared an experience which revolted their souls, and they each felt a need to do something about it, for once, to right a grievous wrong.

When they stopped that first night to camp, they ate very little and talked even less. They slept a few hours and started out again early, while the sky was still dark and filled with stars. Davis wondered if somewhere up there in the heavens a Divine Providence looked down on them, and if so, he wondered, what did it think about human activity? Was it indifferent to human greed and human suffering? If not, why did it seem never to interfere to protect the innocent?

The sun was low in the eastern sky when Chato raised his arm and the four riders halted. He pointed almost straight ahead toward the foothills they were approaching. A slim column of smoke rose into the cool early morning air.

"That looks like chimney smoke," said Sieber.

They rode ahead and came to a small cantina, an adobe with dilapidated walls. They dismounted and tied their horses to the hitching rail in front. There were a few horses already there, and there were others in the small corral beside the building.

Inside it was dark. The floor was dirt. There were small wooden tables and a simple wood bar. It was not a place of entertainment, just a place to get drunk and, maybe, to forget about the heat. Gatewood stepped in, followed by Sieber, Chato, and Davis. They moved to the bar.

"Buscando a un hombre," said Gatewood, "Diego Redondo."

The bartender looked across the room to an alcove. Gatewood followed his gaze and saw there a seated *vaquero* wearing a long serape and a straw hat. He couldn't see the man's face.

"Mr. Davis," he said.

He started toward the alcove with Davis following. Sieber leaned his elbows on the bar.

"Tequila, por favor," he said.

The bartender put a glass in front of Sieber and poured it full of tequila. Sieber took the glass and raised it to his lips.

Gatewood and Davis stopped by the table in the alcove, and a voice came out from under the wide brim of the straw hat.

"¿Usted es Señor Gatewood?"

"Yes," said Gatewood. "You speak American?"

"I am an American," said the *vaquero*, leaning forward as Gatewood and Davis took seats across from him. "At least I was."

He pushed back his hat to reveal a darkened face sporting a long mustache, but a face with clearly American features. Davis pulled a small bag out of his pocket and handed it across the table.

"Tobacco?" he said.

The *vaquero* took the bag.

"I've been here more than twenty years," he said. "I was in the war. Confederate officer. After the hostilities ended, I went to Texas, got into a little scrape there with the law, came down here, got a new name, new start, wife, family. But in my heart, well, hell, I'm still a Tennessee man."

He poured himself another tequila and downed it at once.

"My wife and her sisters," he said, "they trade with Apache women come down from the mountains. They've done it for years."

He paused, and Gatewood put a twenty dollar gold piece on the table. Still the *vaquero* hesitated. Gatewood put down another coin.

"A few days back," said the *vaquero*, "some Chiricahua showed up near here."

Gatewood put down three more coins.

"Where?" he said.

"Straight up Montana Avviripe," said the *vaquero*, and he finished off his tequila.

At the bar, Chato and Sieber watched as the door opened to let six men in. The leader of the six spotted a waitress and yelled out to her.

"*Copas.*"

"Si, Señor," said the waitress.

The leader was wearing a black hat with a hawk feather in the band. He, like four of the others, was a white man. The sixth was Indian. All were dirty, scruffy, a rough looking bunch. They moved to a table behind where Sieber stood at the bar, and four of them sat down. The remaining two, one of them the Indian, took their places at the bar, on either side of Chato.

Back in the alcove Gatewood watched the six men. He knew who they were. Sieber, at the bar, also watched as he drank. The *vaquero* got up from the table and walked out of the cantina, passing by Sieber on his way to the door. The waitress took a bottle and glasses to the four men at the table and then went out into the kitchen. Sieber turned to face the ringleader.

"Buenos dias," he said. "I didn't expect to run into many Americans down here. Where you fellows from?"

The leader looked up at Sieber and smiled, revealing white teeth underneath his dark mustache. He appeared to be about forty years old.

"Texas," he said. "I keep a house in Brewster County."

"Awful far from home, ain't you?" said Sieber.

"We come down here to try to make a living," said the gang leader. The others smiled broadly at the comment.

"How about you, friend?" asked the Texan. "Seems you got a real curious nature. You the law?"

"Me?" said Sieber. "Hell, no. I'm hunting that son of a bitch Geronimo. Thought maybe you all might have come across something that'd help me out."

"Sorry, amigo," said the Texan. "We ain't seen nothing."

He drank down a shot of liquor and leaned over toward the man on his left. They talked for a moment in low voices, looking up at Chato. Sieber turned away from them and spat on the floor. The Texan pushed back his chair and stood up, still looking at Chato.

"You Apache?" he asked.

Chato nodded.

"You sit down here," said the Texan, "while we have us a drink. We'll take real good care of you."

The Indian standing next to Chato shoved a revolver into Chato's side. Chato, the other Indian keeping the gun barrel pressed into his side, moved over to the table. The two of them sat down.

Gatewood and Davis stood up from their table in the alcove.

"Mr. Davis," said Gatewood.

"Sir?"

With a nod of his head, Gatewood indicated the door to the kitchen on the other side of the room.

"Cover my back," he said. "Anything happens, fire and keep firing."

"Yes sir," said Davis. He walked over to the kitchen door, as Gatewood headed for the front door of the cantina. Passing close by Sieber, Gatewood spoke in a low voice.

"Al."

"It's them," said Sieber.

Gatewood kept moving until he came to a spot

between the door and the Texan's table. He turned to face the Texan.

"That Apache's with us," said Sieber.

"Don't look like it to me," said the Texan.

"He's a sergeant of scouts in the United States Army," said Gatewood.

"Who the hell are you?" demanded the Texan, whirling to face Gatewood.

"Lieutenant Charles Gatewood, Sixth Cavalry."

"You boys are out of uniform," said the Texan. He looked over at Chato. "Maybe he ought to wear one. Somebody down here might take that scalp of his. Make themselves a little money. But I can tell you, you ought to be extra careful around here. Lots of banditos up in them mountains. Real bad hombres."

"Ten days ago," said Gatewood, "we came across a Yaqui village. Most of the Indians were dead. Slaughtered."

"We ran into the same type of thing awhile back," said the Texan. "This here's a crazy country."

"One hundred dollars buys our friend back," said Gatewood. He tossed a bag of gold coins onto the table, and the Texan picked it up, hefted it and stuffed it into a pocket.

"Nice doing business with you, Mr. Gatewood," the Texan said, "but I still admire this Apache's head of hair."

"You rotten son of a bitch," said Sieber. "You took the money."

The scalphunter left standing at the bar moved his hand toward his revolver.

"Amigo," he said, a warning in his voice. Sieber saw him out of the corner of his eye. There was one to his left and five at the table in front of him.

"We made a deal," said Gatewood.

"I changed my mind," said the Texan. "Now you boys are lucky. I'm going to let you walk out of here. Start moving, Dixie-boy."

Gatewood sighed and moved as if to leave. Then he turned suddenly, drawing his revolver and firing. The Texan fell backward with a hole in his chest. There followed a moment of stunned silence. Then everyone seemed to move and to start firing at once. Sieber drew his revolver and fired a shot into the side of the man at the bar. The Indian who had been holding a gun on Chato sucked in his breath in pain and surprise and looked down to see where Chato had sunk his knife in between the ribs. Bullets sank into the wall behind Gatewood and nicked the bar, causing the bartender to drop to the floor behind it. Bottles broke over his head. A shot from Gatewood's revolver hit another of the scalphunters at the table, and the man next to him jumped up and ran toward the kitchen, but Davis, still standing by the kitchen door, fired two shots and dropped him.

Suddenly all was quiet. Smoke and the smell of gunpowder filled the little room. The six scalphunters lay dead on the floor. Gatewood stood staring blankly ahead. Chato got up to move over to his side. Squinting through the smoke, Davis saw that Sieber was down. He ran over to kneel beside the scout. Putting a hand behind him to help him sit up, he felt the hot, sticky blood, and he pulled the hand away again and looked at it. He looked back at Sieber.

"God damn," said Sieber. "Never thought I'd get killed trying to help an Apache."

"We got them all, Mr. Sieber," said Davis. "We got them all."

Gatewood, having shaken off his stunned state, stepped over to stand behind Davis. He looked over Davis's shoulder at Sieber.

"Hell," said Sieber, "I've been gun shot, arrow shot, seventeen times. Been twenty years chasing old Geronimo. I'd love nothing better than being there at the finish."

"You don't have to account for yourself to me, Al," said Gatewood. "You're a brave man."

Sieber smiled.

"I never did have no kind of luck," he said. "I think I'll catch me a little sleep. Rotten sons of bitches."

He closed his eyes as his head fell gently to one side, and he was dead.

Davis and Gatewood stood at the base of a mountain, three pack burros trailing them. A short distance away, Chato was conferring with several Mexican peons. The two officers stared at the mountains looming ahead of them. They had moved high up into the Sierra Madres, and along the way, they had traded their mules for the burros.

Following the lead of the *vaquero* in the cantina, they had located Mount Avviripe. The local peons had confirmed the *vaquero*'s tale. Then they heard that two women from Geronimo's band had been in a nearby town the day before, bartering for food. Their trading done, they had disappeared up Mount Avviripe. Suddenly, after so long a trail, they had known they were close.

Chato broke away from the conversation with the peons and walked back to where Gatewood and Davis waited. "They say the trail starts there," Chato said, pointing. "We leave the horses behind. Go on foot with the burros."

Gatewood continued staring at the mountain as Chato talked.

The trail up the mountain was narrow and steep, often bordering on a deep gorge with a sheer drop to jagged rocks a thousand feet below. Davis, Gatewood, and Chato led the burros as far as they could up the treacherous path. Then the trail narrowed, and Gatewood, in the lead, began half crawling, hand over hand. He heard the burros braying their protests from behind him, and he turned to look over his shoulder in time to see the trailing burro slip, fall over the edge, and plummet a thousand feet into the canyon below, and he felt a sensation like the pit of his stomach dropping out and falling along with the wretched animal.

He took a deep breath and continued to move forward. Davis and Chato, following him, imitated his half crawling movements. The trail continued to twist and wind its way upward. At last they came to a spot with enough flat ground to stop for a rest. Chato looked upward. The trail was becoming yet narrower and steeper.

"Gatewood," said Chato. "No more burros. They can't go higher."

Gatewood turned to face Davis. "From here on," he said, "Chato and I will go on alone. You stay here with the animals."

"Sir," said Davis, "are you giving me a choice?"

"No, Lieutenant," said Gatewood. "I'm giving you an order. I know it's hard to come this far and then stop. I'm sorry. But from here on it's between me and Geronimo. There's no point in getting you killed for nothing."

He reached out with his open right hand toward Davis, who took it in his own for a warm handshake. For a brief moment they looked into each other's eyes.

"Good luck, sir," said Davis.

Gatewood stood up to get moving again, and Chato followed his lead. Davis moved over to stand beside the burros, looking and feeling abandoned. Gatewood started to climb, then paused to look back over his shoulder at Davis.

"If we don't come back," he said, "write to my wife. Tell her—we're trying to make a country out here, and it's hard. Tell her I love her. Tell her I love my children."

He turned to resume his climb.

Davis suddenly felt very much alone. He asked himself what he would do should he never see Gatewood and Chato alive again, and he found that he had no answer. How long should he wait before assuming the worst? He did not know. His career in the military, short though it had been, had not turned out to be what he had expected. He found himself engaged, for the most part, in activities which were repugnant to his own sense of right and wrong. The only thing he had done so far that felt good and proper had been an act of murder, and the only men he found that he could admire were also capable of ruthless action. He wondered if he would die with his mind still in a muddle, alone on the side of this mountain.

Higher up, the distance from the trail to the rocks below had increased to thousands of feet. The sun beat down unmercifully. Gatewood had discarded his military blouse, and his longjohn tops were sweaty, dirty, and torn. A small cross which hung on a thin chain around his neck was visible, swinging loose. Feeling that they must be getting close, Gatewood paused long enough to tie a white handkerchief to the muzzle end of his rifle.

He struggled to get over the edge and up onto a small terrace. Chato had moved ahead and was up above on top of a rock formation. He reached a dark brown hand down toward Gatewood, and Gatewood took it, then felt himself being pulled up and over the rocks. On top, he stumbled to his feet. Standing side by side, Gatewood and Chato looked upward and around. They found themselves surrounded by armed Apaches. Standing foremost among them was Mangas, and he held his rifle pointed directly at Chato.

Chapter 17

It was a tense moment. Gatewood thought that it was probably the most dangerous situation he had ever found himself in, and if he managed to live through it, he hoped never to see another like it. And he realized, too, that he had put Chato in the same precarious situation as himself, perhaps even worse, for the Apaches saw Gatewood as an enemy, but they looked on Chato as a traitor. Mangas stared hard at Chato and held his rifle steady, aimed at Chato's chest.

"Why did you bring him?" Mangas asked Gatewood. "He's an enemy to his own people."

"He thinks you are," said Gatewood.

Mangas raised his rifle as if to shoot, and Gatewood spoke again quickly.

"He's a brave man to come here," Gatewood said. "Enough Chiricahuas are dead."

Ulzana jumped down from the rocks to stand on the same level with Gatewood and Chato. He stepped over to Gatewood and swung his rifle butt, smashing Gatewood on the side of the head and knocking him to the ground.

"Ah."

Gatewood groaned and involuntarily reached for the side of his head, and he felt the warm sticky blood on the palm of his hand.

"Enough Chiricahuas are dead because the White-eyes killed them," said Ulzana. "You killed them."

"My family," said Mangas. "All of them are dead."

Gatewood thought that it was all over. He was waiting for the bullet that would end his life. Then suddenly Geronimo appeared, stepping up from behind the warriors who stood alongside Mangas. He looked down on Gatewood and Chato.

"Enough," Geronimo said. Ulzana stepped back, grudgingly, and Geronimo laid down his rifle, made his way down from the rocks, and walked over to Gatewood. Gatewood looked up, squinting. One eye was swollen and bloody.

"Are you hurt bad?" asked Geronimo.

"No," said Gatewood, rising uneasily to his feet and slowly straightening himself up to face Geronimo. He was still a soldier, and he was on a special assignment. He had to appear as bold and dignified as he could, even though he was tired, dirty, and hurt. "It'll mend," he said.

"Come over here," said Geronimo. "Let's sit down and talk." He led the way to a flat rock, long and low like a bench. They sat down side by side, and Geronimo called for water and a rag for Gatewood's head.

"So," Geronimo said, as Gatewood daubed at the side of his head, "we haven't talked for a while. How are things with you?"

"I've been all right," said Gatewood. "They've kept me at a desk."

"And how are things back home with the Chiricahuas?"

Gatewood looked at the ground between his feet.

"There are no Chiricahuas left in Arizona," he said. "They've all been sent to Florida."

"Because of me?" asked Geronimo.

"Yes," said Gatewood. "I think so. Because of you." There was a moment of silence. Gatewood felt the side of his head begin to throb.

"I knew you would come, Gatewood," said Geronimo. "I've been waiting for you here."

"I bring an offer," said Gatewood, "from the new White-eye chief, General Miles, to stop the killing."

"The White-eye chiefs make many offers," said Geronimo. "Still the Apaches are driven from their land. Still the Apaches are killed. Have they now taught you to lie, Gatewood?"

Gatewood pointed toward the warriors standing around.

"Look and see," he said, "how few warriors you have left. General Miles will hunt you down if it takes fifty years. He has already sent your families to Florida."

"Tell me about this Miles, Gatewood," said Geronimo. "How is his voice to listen to? Is he cruel or kind? When he speaks to you, where does he look? When he makes you a promise, can you trust him to keep his word?

"I need your advice, Gatewood. Consider yourself to be one of us and not a white man. Remember all that has been said and all that has happened, and, as an Apache, what would you advise me to do?"

"I would trust General Miles," said Gatewood, "and take him at his word."

The advice was good, Gatewood knew, even if he had not told the whole truth. Geronimo and the others were doomed if they did not surrender. Geronimo stood up and stepped around to stand in front of Gatewood.

"If I kill White-eyes forever," he said, "I am still Geronimo, an Apache. Who are you, Gatewood?"

"I m a warrior," said Gatewood, "a man like you. We can die here, you and me, or we can live. Either way, the killing must stop. The war must end."

He reached up and took hold of the cross which hung from the chain around his neck. He closed his fist tight over it and gave a jerk, breaking the chain. Then he held it out in the palm of his hand for Geronimo to look at.

"My God is a God of peace," he said, "of life, not death. What does your God say?"

Geronimo looked at the cross for a moment.

"The Apache God is a God of peace," he said. "Tell me what is in your heart."

"The war is over," said Gatewood, and he handed the cross to Geronimo. "I offer this," he said, "because it has power for me. Our fight must end here. Now tell me what is in your heart."

Holding the cross, Geronimo turned to look into the faces of his men. Some were filled with hate. All were tired and grim. Then his eyes swept the mountains and the sky around them.

"When I was young, I took a wife," he said. "We lived in these mountains. We had our family. The Mexican soldiers came and killed her. They killed her and my two little girls. Killed them because we are Apache. There was no other reason for it. We were trading with those people. We were friendly."

He paused, his thoughts lost in long ago, his feelings caught up by those thoughts and the painful memories they brought back.

"I remember when I found their bodies," he said. "I stood until much time had passed, not knowing what I would do. I had no weapon, but I did not want to fight. I did not pray. I did not do anything. I had no purpose left.

"After a year had passed, my power showed me how to get revenge. Always since then, I have got revenge. But no matter how many I kill, I can not bring back my family."

He paused for a moment, looking off in the distance. His eyes were wet with tears, but no tears fell. He held up Gatewood's cross and looked at it again. Then he turned back toward Gatewood.

"I gave you the blue stone," he said. "You gave me this. It will be peace."

He turned and slowly walked away.

Gatewood and Davis rode with Geronimo and what was left of his band back into Arizona Territory. Chato had ridden ahead to report to General Miles, who made immediate preparations to meet them. As Geronimo and his escort rode up onto a mountain plateau, they saw coming toward them a long line of cavalry and infantry. The Apaches stopped and waited, proud and defiant. The cavalry rode up within a few yards and halted. Miles himself sat on his horse in front of the line.

Geronimo looked at Miles for a moment, dismounted, and walked forward. Miles dismounted to wait for the Apache leader. When Geronimo drew close to Miles, he pulled a revolver and a bowie knife out of his belt and held them forward.

"I want to surrender with all my people," he said. "I'll do as you say and go where you tell me to go—or send me. I'm tired of the warpath, and my people are all worn out."

Miles took the weapons in his own hands.

"Geronimo," he said, "I accept your surrender."

He made a sweeping movement with his right arm and an army wagon drove forward. Miles gestured toward the wagon, and he and Geronimo walked over to it.

"Florida for two years," he said. "You and the other Apaches must make a new life."

Miles climbed into the wagon and indicated to Geronimo that he wanted him to follow. Geronimo took a last look around at the surrounding desert and mountains. He looked back at Miles.

"I give myself up to you," he said. "Do with me what you please. Once I moved about like the wind. Now I surrender to you, and that is all."

He climbed into the wagon with Miles, and the wagon pulled away, followed by the massive military escort. Gatewood and Davis remained behind. They watched the Apaches they had brought in being led across the desert.

"It's over, Mr. Davis," said Gatewood. "I've been reassigned by the general. I'm to have no further duties in Arizona Territory. I leave tomorrow."

They watched the Chiricahua band and its military escort slowly diminish on the horizon. Gatewood extended his hand, and Davis took it in his.

"It's been my pleasure," said Gatewood. "I hope to serve with you again in the future."

Gatewood turned away and mounted his brown cavalry charger, then stared after the wagon, up ahead with the military column. He knew that he would never again see Geronimo. He looked back at Davis and touched the brim of his hat, then turned his horse and rode away.

Geronimo was held at San Carlos for several weeks. Gatewood had been transferred to Wyoming. The army, unable to defeat Geronimo by traditional means, still chose to overlook the efforts of Gatewood. Instead of being rewarded with a medal, he was sentenced to obscurity.

From inside the stockade, Geronimo watched through barred windows as an officer appeared on the headquarters porch and walked down toward fifty assembled Apache scouts. Mounted cavalry was deployed at the back and to the sides of the standing Apache soldiers.

"Attention," called the sergeant major.

The scouts snapped to attention.

"Present arms," called the sergeant major.

The scouts executed the maneuver, and troopers began moving down the line to collect the rifles from the scouts. When they had almost finished, an officer stepped front and center and held out an official document.

"By order of the office of the President of the United States," he read, "all Chiricahua scouts are under arrest and will be transported to Fort Pickens Prison, Pensacola, Florida, along with the outlaw Apaches led by—Gokhlaye—"

He stumbled awkwardly over the pronunciation of the Apache word, then continued reading.

"—known as Geronimo.

"The Apache scouts from the White Mountain, Coyotero, and Mescalero tribes are to return at once to their reservations. They will remain within these boundaries unless given express permission to travel. Their duties for the United States Army are at an end. We thank them for their service."

Finished, the officer wheeled and headed back for the headquarters building. Chato stood in the ranks of the scouts, his rifle still in his hands. A trooper stepped in front of him.

"Give me that rifle, Sergeant," said the trooper.

"I'm a good Apache," said Chato. "This is not right."

The trooper jerked the rifle roughly from Chato's hands. "Shut the hell up," he said, "and stay in line."

"I'm a good Apache," protested Chato. "I'm Sergeant Chato, a scout."

The trooper, having moved on, glanced back at Chato.

"Maybe you want to talk to the president," he said, "huh, Chato?"

Geronimo watched through his barred window. Now they would know, he thought. Now they would realize that they should have listened to him. He had warned his own followers that if they surrendered, they would be put in prison. They would not be returned to their reservation. But, unbelievably, the White-eyes were even worse than what Geronimo had thought. They were even arresting those Apaches who had been their friends, who had helped track down their own people. Now they would know.

The following day, Geronimo, his band of so-called renegades, and all the Chiricahua scouts who had served in the army were loaded into wagons and transported to Holbrook, Arizona, where they were to be put on a military train to Florida.

Lieutenant Davis watched from the window of the squad room as the wagons loaded with the Chiricahuas moved out from San Carlos, and he felt his jaws tighten involuntarily. He turned from the window and walked over to the desk of an aide-de-camp.

"Mr. Glenville," he said, "I'd like to see the general."

Glenville was shuffling papers. He didn't even bother to look up at Davis. "On what business?" he said.

"It's about Mr. Gatewood," said Davis.

Glenville stood up and walked around the desk and over to the door that led to General Miles's office. He opened the door and waited, standing at attention.

Inside the office, Miles looked up from behind his desk. "Yes?" he said.

"Mr. Davis, sir," said Glenville, "about Mr. Gatewood."

"All right, Glenville," said Miles, with an impatient sigh. "Send him in."

Davis walked past Glenville, paused and gathered himself up, then stepped smartly over to stop in front of the general's desk.

"Sir," he said, "I thought the United States Army kept its word. I thought maybe we were the only ones left who did. What's going on out there is a disgrace."

"That's quite enough, Lieutenant," said Miles, taking off his glasses. "I don't know if I'm talking to an officer in the United States Army or to a dangerously simple-minded man. You're more worried about keeping your word to a savage than you are of fulfilling your duty to the citizens of this country. We won. That's what matters. It's over,

Lieutenant. Geronimo. The Apaches. Over. I suppose the whole history of the West is over—except for being a farmer." He said that last with a tone of disgust in his voice, as he picked up his glasses and put them back on, took up his pen again, and went back to writing, back to business. Then as if he had just remembered, he looked up again at Davis. "You wanted to see me about Gatewood," he added.

"Yes sir," said Davis. "I don't think Mr. Gatewood would want me to be any part of this, sir—the betrayal of our Apache scouts."

"I hate an idealist," said Miles. "There's always something messy about an idealist. But I understand that a lot of people are born that way."

He stopped writing and looked up at Davis again.

"I'll give you some advice, son," Miles said. "Get out of the army. You're not cut out for it."

"Sir," said Davis, "I'm ashamed, and you have my resignation."

He gave his last snappy salute, turned, and walked out of the office, anxious to divest himself of the blue uniform which he had once been so proud to wear.

A train chugged across the open, empty sea of grass of the Texas plains leaving a long trail of black smoke dissolving into a dark sky. In a cattle car crowded with Apaches, Geronimo sat next to Mangas. Across the way Chato sat on the floor of the car, his knees drawn up to his chest. Armed troopers watched over all.

"You were right to fight them," said Chato,

speaking his own tongue. "Everything they promised me was a lie."

"You helped them kill Apaches," said Mangas. "I will despise you until I die."

Geronimo looked at Chato, then at Mangas. "There are so few Chiricahuas left," he said. "They should not hate each other."

He heard a cough and looked in the direction of the sound. A young Apache woman holding a baby in her arms looked very sick. She suddenly fell victim to a long fit of deep coughing.

"She has the coughing sickness," said Geronimo. "She'll die soon. Maybe the baby, too."

He paused, listening to the noises of the iron wheels on the iron tracks beneath him and to the clacking and clanking of the moving cars. The engineer blew the whistle, and Geronimo thought that it had a particularly lonesome and eerie quality to its sound.

"No one knows," he said, "why the one God let the White-eyes come here and take what was ours. Why did there have to be so many of them? Why did they have so many guns and so many soldiers and so many horses? For many years the one God made me a warrior. No gun, no bullets would ever kill me. That was my power. Now my time is over. Now, maybe the time of our people is over."

Mangas looked at Geronimo and then lowered his head, as if in shame, or deep sadness, or both. Geronimo looked through the slats of the cattle car at the country passing by.

Epilogue

Geronimo was taken from San Carlos to San Antonio, Texas, where he narrowly escaped being tried in civilian court for his "crimes" and was held in jail for forty days. The newspapers were filled with horror stories regarding the "atrocities" perpetrated by this "cruel, inhuman monster." (Even the President of the United States, Grover Cleveland, wanted to see him hanged for murder.) From there he was taken on to Fort Pickens, Florida, where he began serving time at hard labor. He and other Apaches were put to work sawing large logs. Although just over thirty Apache men had been "hostile" at the time of Geronimo's final surrender, the United States government had the entire Chiricahua band of 498 men, women, and children rounded up and sent to Florida.

The climate of the humid southeast was not healthy for the Apaches, and many of them sickened and died. One man shot and killed both his wife and himself. More than one hundred Apaches died in Florida. In addition, their children were taken away from them and sent to school at Carlisle, Pennsylvania, where fifty of the children, including two of Chato's, died.

Back in Arizona, old Eskiminzin, who had always only wanted to live in peace, where he could make his *tiswin,* was arrested on a charge of "communicating" with the outlaw Apache Kid, and he and the Aravaipas were collected and shipped off to Florida with the rest.

After two years of misery in Florida, during which time they had not seen their families, in spite of the promises made by General Miles, the Apaches were transferred to Mount Vernon Barracks, Alabama, in May of 1887. There they were again put to work at hard labor for the government. They had been lied to again. They did not go home to Arizona after their two years in Florida. They did not receive their promised land allotments. They did not receive farm implements or livestock.

In August of 1894, after nine years in Florida and Alabama, the Apaches were finally sent back west, but not far enough west, not back to their old homes. They were sent to Fort Sill, in what is now southern Oklahoma, where they remained prisoners of war. There they were given small houses, cattle, hogs, turkeys, and chickens. They were put to work farming on a small scale.

There at Fort Sill, the Apaches did become

successful at raising cattle, but they did not do so well with the other creatures. They were allowed to sell the cattle they raised and keep part of the money. The rest was put into an "Apache fund." Geronimo complained about the management of the money.

In 1898, Geronimo was visited at Fort Sill by General Miles, and he asked the former crockery store clerk to use his influence to allow him to go home.

"The acorns and piñon nuts," he said, "the quail and the wild turkey, the giant cactus and the palo verdes—they all miss me. I miss them, too. I want to go back to them."

General Miles laughed at the old warrior.

"A very beautiful thought, Geronimo," he said. "Quite poetic. But the men and women who live in Arizona, they do not miss you. Folks in Arizona sleep now at night. They have no fear that Geronimo will come and kill them. The acorns and piñon nuts will have to get along as best they can without you."

Geronimo also asked the general to see to it that he was excused from any further forced labor because of his age. (He was 69 years old.) Miles did so, and from then on, Geronimo worked when he felt like it. The old warrior also eventually adopted Christianity, or at least, pretended to, joining the Dutch Reformed Church in 1903. (He was later expelled because of his love of gambling.)

In 1904, he was invited by members of the Indian Bureau to be taken to the St. Louis World's Fair, and after receiving assurances that he would be protected and that the President of the United States had said that it was all right, he agreed.

At the fair, he sold copies of his photograph for twenty-five cents each and was allowed to keep ten cents from each sale for himself. He had also learned to write his name, and he sold autographs for ten, fifteen, and twenty-five cents, keeping all of that money. He rode in a Ferris wheel, and he had his picture taken in an automobile.

In 1905, he rode in the inauguration parade of President Theodore Roosevelt, because Roosevelt "wanted to give the people a good show." Geronimo was actually able, on that occasion, to visit with the president, and he took advantage of the situation to present the following plea:

"Great Father, I look to you as I look to God. When I see your face, I think I see the face of the Great Spirit. I come here to pray you to be good to me and my people.

"I fought to protect my homeland. Did I fear the Great White Chief? No. He was my enemy and the enemy of my people. His people desired the country of my people. My heart was strong against him. I said that he should never have my country. I defied the Great White Chief, for in those days, I was a fool. I had a bad heart.

"I ask you to think of me as I was then. I lived in the home of my people. They trusted me. It was right that I should give them my strength and my wisdom.

"When the soldiers of the Great White Chief drove me and my people from our home, we went into the mountains. When they followed us, we slew all that we could. We said we would not be captured. No. We starved, but we killed. I said that we would never yield, for I was a fool.

"So I was punished, and all my people were punished with me. The white soldiers took me and made me a prisoner far from my own country.

"Great Father, other Indians have homes where they can live and be happy. I and my people have no homes. The place where we are kept is bad for us. We are sick there, and we die. White men are in the country that was my home. I pray you to tell them to go away and let my people go there and be happy.

"Great Father, my hands are tied as with a rope. My heart is no longer bad. I will tell my people to obey no chief but the Great White Chief. I pray you to cut the ropes and make me free. Let me die in my own country, an old man who has been punished enough and is free."

Unlike Miles, Roosevelt did not laugh. He was sympathetic, but the answer he gave to Geronimo was essentially the same as the one that Miles had given. The white people of Arizona would not stand for it.

Later that same year, Mr. S. M. Barrett, a white man, then Superintendent of Education in Lawton, Oklahoma, secured permission from Roosevelt to interview Geronimo and get him to tell his life story. Geronimo told the tale in the Apache language to Asa Daklugie, the son of Whoa who translated it into English for Barrett to write down. Then, at Geronimo's insistence, the process was reversed. Barrett read his manuscript to Daklugie, who then translated it back into Apache for Geronimo's final approval.

Geronimo was bitter in his old age and regretted that he had surrendered to Miles rather than fight it out to the end. He wanted more than anything else in life to be allowed to return to his homeland, and in telling his tale, he omitted most of the details regarding his problems with the United States and concentrated instead on stories of fighting the Mexicans. He also dedicated the book to President Theodore Roosevelt.

He was never to realize his last dream. On February 17, 1909, he died at Fort Sill, technically, still a prisoner of war. He was about eighty years old.

The rest of the Apaches were kept at Fort Sill until 1911, when they were allowed to return to New Mexico. A number of them made the move and settled at Mescalero. Two years later, one hundred eighty-seven more joined them there, leaving only about one hundred in Oklahoma. These were almost all younger people who chose to stay in the new state. It was the only home many of them had ever known.

Nana and Geronimo were dead, buried in Oklahoma, but Naiche made it home to die peacefully of old age. Of the old scouts, Chato and Noche at least made it home in time to die, both of them leaving this earth in 1914. Geronimo's son Robert became a successful New Mexico stock raiser. (Over the years, Geronimo had remarried five times. He never, he said, had more than one wife at a time.) Asa Daklugie lived at Mescalero until his death there in 1955.

General George Crook managed to hang on to his reputation as a soldier that the Indians trusted. So, in 1889, he was sent back to the northern plains to negotiate away thousands of acres of land at $1.50 an acre from the Sioux. At last he had his victory. What he had been unable to do on the battlefield, he did at the negotiating table. With the opposition of Sitting Bull, Hollow Horn Bear, High Hawk, Yellow Hair, Crow Dog, and the great Red Cloud, Crook managed the breakup of the Great Sioux Reservation. He died of a heart attack in 1890.

Nelson Miles, on the other hand, the clerk who had purchased his original commission, commanded the forces that massacred the men, women, and children of Big Foot's band of Sioux at Wounded Knee in 1890. He also commanded the troops that were sent to Chicago in 1894 to put down the Pullman Strike. In 1895, he was appointed Commander of the United States Army, and in 1898, he led the forces that defeated the Spanish in Puerto Rico. He retired in 1903 and died in Washington, D.C., in 1925.

Two years after Geronimo's surrender to General Miles, Lieutenant Charles B. Gatewood was seriously injured at Fort McKinney, Wyoming. He was trying to put out a fire when a powder magazine blew up. He died soon after. His wife and their two children back in Virginia were given a pension of seventeen dollars a month.

Britton Davis's resignation was accepted by Miles, presumably without regrets. Davis abandoned his hopes for a military career and became a manager of ranches and mining ventures.

Apaches continued to live on reservations in Arizona, New Mexico, and Oklahoma. They live in those places to this day. And the story of Gokhlaye, known to the world as Geronimo, grew steadily into legend. In the press, he was a heartless savage and a madman. In dime novels he became a monster. Later, comic books picked up the wild tales, and then, of course, Hollywood.

Geronimo has been depicted in numerous motion pictures, almost always as a villain. In Paramount's 1939 film *Geronimo,* the title role was played by Chief Thundercloud (Victor Daniels of Muskogee, Oklahoma, who was a Cherokee), although the actual star of the film was Preston Foster. In 1950, Jay Silverheels played him at odds with Cochise in 20th Century-Fox's *Broken Arrow.* And much has been made of Chuck Connors's blue-eyed Geronimo in the 1962 United Artists film entitled *Geronimo.* In these films and many others, either Geronimo has been portrayed as a villain, or the film has been ludicrous, or both.

Columbia Pictures 1993 *Geronimo: An American Legend,* starring full-blood Cherokee actor Wes Studi, gives us a long overdue, balanced portrait of the great patriot warrior.

About the Author

ROBERT J. CONLEY was born in Cushing, Oklahoma, in 1940. He received a bachelor's degree in drama and art and a master's degree in English from Midwestern University. He has taught English at Northern Illinois University, Southwest Missouri State University, and Morningside College. He has also served as director of Indian Studies at Eastern Montana College and as assistant programs manager for the Cherokee Nation of Oklahoma.

Since the publication of his first novel in 1986, Mr. Conley has written sixteen novels and a collection of short stories. He received the 1988 Spur Award for Best Short Story from the Western Writers of America for "Yellow Bird: An Imaginary Autobiography," and won the 1992 Spur Award for Best Western Novel for *Nickajack*. Among his other works acclaimed for their unique voice and Cherokee perspective are *Go-Ahead Rider, Strange Company, The Way of the Priests*, and *Mountain Windsong*, which Tony Hillerman said "is beautiful and heartwarming as well as tragic. . . . *Mountain Windsong* deserves to become an American classic."

Robert J. Conley lives in Oklahoma with his wife, Evelyn, also Cherokee. He now writes full time, and his new *Go-Ahead Rider* novel, *To Make a Killing*, will be available from Pocket Books next month.